I0592884

Her Outback Protector

Annie Seaton

Second Chance Bay Series

Her Outback Playboy

Her Outback Protector

Her Outback Haven

Her Outback Paradise

ANNIE SEATON

ISBN 9780648399087

DEDICATION

This book is dedicated to Ian, my patient husband. It was written very quickly, and he cooked while I wrote!

ANNIE SEATON

ACKNOWLEDGEMENTS

A special thank you to:
my wonderful editor and critique partner, Susanne Bellamy, and my eagle-eyed proof-reader, Roby Aiken

Chapter 1

As the small plane banked to the right Claire Templeton leaned forward and pressed her face to the window. For the first time in three days of travelling and gradually changing her appearance in cheap motel rooms, a glimmer of confidence began deep within her.

Brisbane to Mackay. Mackay to Cairns. Cairns to Mt Isa.

And now the final leg of her trip to Second Chance Bay at the base of the Gulf of Carpentaria was almost over.

Maybe she'd done it. Claire hoped she had; her future depended on it.

She jumped as the voice of the pilot crackled into her headphones. 'You're in luck today, folks.'

The plane was small, and he'd handed each of the three passengers a set of headphones as they'd boarded in Mt Isa. It suited her; it meant she didn't have to interact with the other passengers, although they both looked harmless enough. An elderly woman clutching half a dozen Myers shopping bags, and a young man who had gone to sleep as soon as the plane had taken off. He didn't stir as the pilot's voice droned on.

'We're over Burketown now, and you can just see the tail end of the Morning Glory. She's late today. Usually passes over Karumba before dawn but if you look to the east'—he turned back to see if they were doing as he instructed— 'you can see those lovely big rolls of cloud.'

Claire peered at the cloud formation. It looked like long rolls of cotton wool. Not very wide but stretching as far as she could see. Quite impressive.

'The Morning Glory is unique to the Gulf of Carpentaria. It's not very wide but can stretch — sometimes in an almost perfectly straight line — for a thousand kilometres from one side of the gulf to the other. Bloody awesome, it is. I never get tired of seeing it.' He turned again and caught Claire's eye with a grin because she was the only one paying attention to him. 'They say the old codgers in the Burketown pub can smell it coming.'

Claire nodded and gave him a polite smile before she looked back to the window.

The plane began to descend, and she turned her attention to the narrow river snaking through the wetlands beneath them. A silver ribbon caught the early morning sun, and to her deep satisfaction, there was not one sign of habitation below.

Claire had researched her destination, very, very carefully. Second Chance Bay was a place that few people visited; it had little to attract it unless you were a fisherman, and she was highly unlikely to run into anyone who had heard of her.

Or so she hoped.

The last three days of keeping her head down and waiting for someone to recognise her had been exhausting. With a contented sigh, she sat back, and ignored the churning nerves in her stomach.

Her new life was ahead.

The airport was tiny; a small fibro shack with a flat roof, and apparently with no one manning it. The pilot taxied the plane to the gate near the fence before he climbed out. He came around, opened the door and lowered the steps. Claire waited until he'd helped the older woman down and watched as she walked over to a waiting car. The young man bounded off, with a 'thanks, mate' to the pilot, before Claire unbuckled her seatbelt and stood, bending her head low as she stepped through the narrow doorway. Her hands were shaking, and she took a deep breath as a blast of moist, cloying heat almost took her breath away.

The pilot stood at the bottom of the steps and lifted a hand to help her, but she waved him away politely.

'Just the one suitcase?' he asked.

Claire nodded. Looking around, she wondered which way she'd have to walk. There was no taxi service at the airport, but she knew there was a general store about a hundred metres away where she would call a taxi to take her to Second Chance Bay. If there wasn't one available, she would walk. It was only about three kilometres along the river to the small house she'd rented on the north shore; that would be her first obstacle overcome.

She shook her head with a slight grin. No, not really the first, probably the hundred and first obstacle that had confronted her over the past three weeks, but she had to let all that go now.

'Are you getting picked up, love?'

'I'm fine, thank you.'

He handed her the suitcase. 'I've got to get going. I've got a fishing charter out of Normanton mid-morning. Taking a group out to Sweers Island.'

Even though she didn't want to engage, Claire's natural politeness kicked in.

'It was a very pleasant flight and thank you for pointing out the cloud.'

'You here for long?' He looked at her curiously, and she immediately regretted her comment.

'Just a short visit.'

'So I'll see you on the Sunday flight?'

She shook her head. 'No, we're driving to Darwin.' The more of a false trail she could leave, the safer it would be on the slim chance that someone did track her to this isolated bay. The blasted media were so persistent, as she well knew.

'Okay, then. Have a good trip. Bloody hot up there this time of the year.'

Claire nodded and picked up her suitcase. He was right. Even though it wasn't far past eight a.m., the sun was beating down on the top of her now-blonde hair. The breeze picked up the loose strands and blew them across her mouth. At work, she'd kept her hair up in an elegant chignon, and rarely wore it down. That had become her signature look, and the studio had hired Marnie, a hairdresser, simply to look after her styling once the show had taken off. She stopped and put her suitcase down and pulled a scrunchie from her pocket and tied the loose strands back; it was difficult because the new style—thanks to manicure scissors in a motel room—had left it a long shaggy cut of different lengths. Marnie would groan if she could see it now.

Once her hair was tied back as best she could get it, Claire pulled a baseball cap onto her head and picked up her bag, before stepping out to the gate in the fence. A flat wide road ran parallel to the water, and there were a few houses edging the road that headed down towards the general store. She could see the store sign at the front. When she heard the plane taxiing out to the runway, she stopped beneath a tree with wide spreading branches and dug into her handbag for her sunglasses.

The road was deserted, and the only sound was the whoosh of the tiny waves breaking onto the sand across the road, and the occasional sound of a motor as boats headed out into the Gulf.

Claire gripped the handle of her suitcase and set off with a determined step.

***

Don Douglas turned onto the road that lead down to the general store at Karumba Point. Dane and Matt had laughed at his new strategy, but he'd argued with them.

'It's worth a try. I'm sick of the bloody employment agencies sending the wrong people out there. What do they think we need up here?'

'Settle down, mate. It's not a drama. If we can't get someone in time, I'll come with you on this trip, and Jenni can come and help too.' Jake had a solution; his lateral thinking had seen him make his first million before he'd come home to Second Chance Bay before his thirtieth birthday.

'I don't expect you to bail me out, Jake. What about little Leni?'

Jake and Jeni's two-year-old loved being on the water, but it wasn't the place for a child out in the Kimberley wilderness. His brother-in-law, Jake, had been a godsend to the family since he'd come back to the Bay. He'd bought into the family business and the old McDougal boats, the *Helen M* and the *Elsie,* had been refurbished. The fishing business had been so good over the past two seasons, Don had been able to take out a business loan and follow his dream, setting up on his own. He'd bought a classic old boat, built by the well-known boat building family who'd been building craft in Brisbane for over a hundred years. He'd refurbished her for two years in his downtime, hiring contractors for the bigger jobs, but had enjoyed restoring the old timber in the saloon and cabins himself. Within a few months on the water, the *Kimberley Adventurer* was fast building a reputation as one of the top cruises in the northern waterways.

He advertised it as the classic adventure tour and had been attracting the wealthier end of the tourist population. That's why he was fussy about the crew he hired. The employment agency in Darwin didn't get it.

Don had thrown the two applications they'd sent into the bin. 'It's not even worth a reply email. A Dutch girl who doesn't speak English, has no experience, and a sixty-year-old man who wants to fish when he's not on duty? Jesus, give me a break. All I want is a hostess. Someone reliable with a bit of class. Someone who can talk to the passengers. Is that such a big ask?' He folded his arms and shook his head. 'So, I'm trying the locals. Maybe one of the school leavers this year. If we can find a local, that would do the trick. And it would be sustainable.'

Jake had shaken his head, but Matt, Don's brother had laughed, putting the thoughts of the family into words.

'Mate, we have a population of five hundred in Karumba, and sixty-two in Second Chance Bay. You know most of them anyway, so what's the point of putting an ad up in the local store? You could think about it all week, and finally realise there's no one suitable here.'

Don slammed the door of his old Toyota ute and strode to the general store. He walked into the crowded shop and stood at the back near the postcard stand waiting as the three staff behind the counter dealt with the breakfast orders of the crowd from the caravan park next door. Finally, there was a lull and Pammy, the store owner waved him over.

'Good to see you, Donny McDougal. Can I do you a bacon and egg roll? With barbeque sauce like you like it?' Her grin was wide.

'Why not.' Don smiled back. 'You got a minute spare, Pam?' Pam Harris had run the store for as long as he could remember.

'For the best-looking man in town, course I have, love. Come outside and I'll have a quick break. Fleur, a bacon and egg roll for one. On the house.'

She pushed open the door and led Don over to the faded pink umbrella shading the green plastic table and chairs at a precarious angle.

'Fleur,' he said with a grin. 'A backpacker?'

Pam shook her head. 'No, my sister's daughter up from Brisbane. She needed a job.'

'That's what I wanted to ask you.' He held up the small white card he'd filled out. 'I'm after staff.'

'Bloody hard up here, mate.' Pam lit the cigarette and blew out a plume of smoke and Don held his breath until it wafted past.

'It is. I've got a tour leaving next Thursday and I need a hostess.' He gestured to the shop. 'What's Fleur's background?'

Pammy shook her head, but a grin spread across her tanned face. 'You're not poaching my staff. Besides, I'm keeping an eye on her. She got herself in a bit of trouble in the city.'

'Fair enough. Can I put this up on your noticeboard?'

Pammy reached out and took the card. She squinted as she read it aloud.

'Host/Hostess wanted for touring the waterways of the Kimberleys on a ten-day wilderness tour. Preference given to an applicant who is seeking a permanent job. Classic boat, with luxury inclusions, sleeps eighteen guests, chef on board. Day trips on excursion tenders and helicopter. Local knowledge preferred but not essential.' She stubbed her cigarette in the glass ashtray on the table. 'Jeez, Donny boy, you've hit the big time. Sounds pretty swanky. Luxury inclusions, hey?'

'I had to take out a decent loan to set it up that way.'

'I'll bet.' She looked up ruefully. 'Just as well I'm not charging you for your brekky. And here I am not able to afford a decent umbrella.'

Don laughed, and a cheeky grin wrinkled Pam's face. 'You're doing okay,' he said.

'I am, but while ever that umbrella puts up some shade, I don't need to waste money on a new one, do I?'

'You're tight, Pammy.'

'But I'm doing well. Listen, I might apply for your job, Donny. Right up my alley, hey?'

'I couldn't afford you. You've got your own little gold mine here.'

'Yeah, it's doing pretty good. But I tell you what, I could do with a holiday.'

'Grey nomie season is almost done.'

She nodded and lit up another cigarette, and Don moved his chair back a fraction. He wasn't a snob, but a bottle-blonde-haired sixty-year-old with a chain-smoking habit wasn't who he was after, no matter how good a person Pammy was.

'Yep, they're starting to move out. Just the stalwarts left down in Dunrootin' Lane down the back of the park.'

Don chuckled. He loved talking to Pammy; you were always guaranteed a smile, and she was a hoot when she'd had a couple of wines at the pub. 'Yeah, our season's almost done too. Fish have been scarce this last couple of weeks; the wet's building early.'

'The glider group's coming into town to ride the Morning Glory next week, and then I'll take a break, I think.' She shot him a glance before she turned away and blew the smoke over her shoulder. 'I was serious, Donny. If you want a hostess, I can do it.'

'Thanks, mate. But you need a break, it's been a busy winter in town.' What he didn't say was that the type of clientele who paid upwards of twenty thousand dollars for ten days of cruising had high expectations. And that was why he didn't want Jake and Jenni to help him out. The age group on the charter wouldn't appreciate a two-year-old in the small confines of the luxury charter.

'Okay. You're a thoughtful bloke, but—' Pammy stopped talking as she gestured up the road. 'There you go. You've put out the call, and here comes someone new to town. The universe is looking out for you, Donny.'

Don looked to where she was gesturing with her cigarette. A slim young woman was walking along the other side of the road, past the pub pulling a small, wheeled suitcase behind her.

'Give me your card. I'll stick it in the window and bring your brekky out. Want a coffee to go with it?'

'How about one of your legendary chocolate milkshakes?'

'With malt?' she asked.

Don nodded. 'Yes please.'

'Done.' She pushed the chair in and Don looked up, watching curiously as the woman approached the store. Her head was down, but occasionally she would lift it and look around, scanning the road and the houses around her as though she were looking for something. As she turned onto the path towards the store, she lifted her head and looked directly at him. He nodded and smiled, but she put her head down and didn't respond.

With a shrug, Don picked up the Normanton weekly newspaper from the table; maybe it was worth putting an ad in that paper. Spread the net to the next town.

The woman carefully placed her suitcase outside the door, and the bell jangled again as she pushed the door open. A waft of icy air blew out of the shop past him along with the aroma of frying bacon. Don rubbed the back of his neck and his fingers came away wet with perspiration; the season was heating up early. He'd checked the charts; the weather next week was shaping up to be good for the tour.

Ten days on the water with three side trips to local waterfalls, and a helicopter trip to a spectacular gorge. He enjoyed the scenic trips rather than the fishing these days; the clients were wealthy and usually easier to please than the fishermen who were chasing the big catch. Organising them and liaising with National Parks, and the indigenous owners of the area, took up a lot of his time, and he'd even thought about hiring an admin assistant. If he continued as skipper on each charter—Dane was his back-up in case of emergency—he was going to have to move across to Wyndham for the whole season next year.

He grinned ruefully. Apart from the year he'd spent at maritime college in Tassie gaining his master's qualification, he'd always lived in the family home.

It was time to spread his wings.

Pammy came out and placed a wrapped-up burger, and a milkshake in an old-fashioned anodized container in front of him. 'I didn't know if you were in a hurry or not.' She gestured to the window with a smile. 'Your ad's up. And you already have some interest.'

Don leaned forward and looked around Pammy. The woman was standing at the window reading the card. As he watched, she pulled out a small notebook and wrote something down. The phone number, he assumed.

'Told ya.' Pammy's smile was gleeful.

'Not a local?' he asked.

She shrugged. 'Haven't seen her around before.' She chuckled, and her laugh was deep and husky. 'And the suitcase is a dead giveaway, ya dork.'

'True.'

'Do you want me to tell her that you're the one doing the hiring?'

Don looked back inside but the woman had disappeared into the shop. 'Why not? I'm getting desperate. If I don't get someone in the next day or two, I'm going to be serving meals, clearing tables and running the bar as well as skippering the charter.'

'Leave it with me, lovely.'

Don waited as Pam went back inside. It was only a minute or so before the bell jangled again, and the blonde-haired woman walked out. She removed her baseball cap and tipped the huge sunglasses onto the top of her head. 'You're Don McDougal?' Her voice was soft, and Don had to lean forward to hear.

Don put the milkshake down, pushed the chair back and stood. 'I am.'

'And you're the one hiring for the charter in the window inside? Is it filled yet?'

He smiled. 'That job card literally went up about a minute before you walked inside. So no, not yet. Are you interested?'

'Perhaps. I'd need to know what skills you require. And also'—she dropped her eyes and broke eye contact— 'I might not be able to get references in time.'

This time when her hand rose to tuck her hair back he noticed the slight tremor in her fingers.

'Sit down. We can chat about it now.' How lucky was he? If she turned out to be suitable, he could go home and stick it into his brothers. He could tell by her words that she had class.

Don walked around the cheap plastic table and pulled the other chair out and waited until she sat.

'Thank you,' she said. 'I guess I'm about to be interviewed, but I haven't had time to get nervous.' She lifted her head and smiled, and Don stared. When she smiled her whole face lit up, and her green eyes glowed with life.

'Two-way street. I can answer your questions first to see if you think it might suit you.' He looked curiously over at the suitcase. 'You've just arrived in town?'

'I have. I came in on the morning flight from Mt Isa.'

'Do you have accommodation booked?'

This time her nod was slow, and she dropped her gaze again. Don's eyes focused on her lips.

'Yes. Not really holiday accommodation. I'm renting in the next town. I came here to see if I could call a taxi to get me there.'

'The next town?' he said with a frown. 'Normanton?'

She looked up again, and the clarity of her eyes struck him again. 'Second Chance Bay.'

'It's not quite a town,' he said slowly.

'I know,' she said simply.

There was silence for a few seconds and she gestured to his burger. 'Please don't let me keep you from your breakfast. It'll be getting cold.'

'Are you eating? Can I get you a coffee?'

'A coffee would be good. Thank you. Flat white.'

Don stood and walked into the shop again, pleased to see the crowd had thinned. He'd been too busy reading the paper to take notice of the comings and goings of the customers. Pammy was standing at the sink, one hand in soapy water, the other holding a coffee.

'A flat white for the lady, please, Pam,' he called above the radio that had been turned up louder.

Pam nodded to the other girl who moved quickly to the coffee machine. 'I'll bring it out to you.'

Don opened the door and his eyes widened when he took in the empty chair. He swivelled around; the suitcase had gone too. With a shrug and the fleeting thought that he mustn't have measured up, he picked up his burger. The disappointment that ran through him was surprising. It didn't have so much to do with filling his hostess position, but more about satisfying his curiosity about the pretty woman moving to Second Chance Bay

The coffee came out at the same time as the suitcase wheels grated on the gravel path at the side of the shop, and the mystery woman reappeared.

'I needed a wash.' She gestured to the facilities between the shop and the caravan park. 'I didn't like to leave my bag out here, but I guess it's a bit different to the city.'

'You could leave your bag on the side of the road all night, and it would still be there in the morning. It's a pretty safe place here.'

On the land, anyway, he thought. Before Don could stand, she gestured for him to stay where he was, and sat opposite him again. He smiled as he settled back and quickly demolished the small burger. He picked up the napkin and wiped his mouth, and the barbeque sauce from his fingers. Pammy was always heavy-handed with the sauce.

'Let's start again.' He held his hand across the table. 'I'm Don McDougal, owner of the *Kimberley Adventurer*. I live around in Second Chance Bay too.'

Her hand was cold in his, and he could feel the slight tremble in her fingers.

'I'm Claire. Claire…Templeton. And I was intending to look for a job in a few days. I just didn't expect to find one on offer so quickly.' She flicked up the sunglasses again and put them on top of her head. Reaching down into her bag, she pulled out a pair of thick dark-rimmed reading glasses and put them on.

Putting her bag on the floor close to her chair, she sat straight in the chair and regarded him, tension obvious in every line of her body.

'Please don't be nervous. We're very casual up here.' Don tried to put her at ease.

'Thank you.' Her stiff shoulders seemed to relax slightly, but she tugged back the hand that he'd forgotten he was still holding. Her fingers were long and narrow, and her skin was soft.

'Well, Claire, let me tell you a little bit about our family business. My brothers, my sister and her husband, and I have a few boats up here, so we hire a lot of staff. Unfortunately, the hostess I'd signed on for the cruise starting next week called yesterday and said her partner wasn't happy about her being on a boat with a male skipper.' He shook his head. 'I don't think he understood what a big vessel we're on. We've got half a dozen crew and eighteen passengers. Anyway, it doesn't matter. The bottom line is, I'm down a hostess. And I need to find one fast.'

'What sort of work does a hostess do?' she asked.

'Um.' Don tried to gather his thoughts. 'A bit of everything. Services the cabins, serves the meals, clears the tables, and most importantly tallies up the bar bill for the guests at the end of the charter.'

'Okay, that sounds like something I could handle.'

'What sort of work do you usually do?'

The expression that crossed her face was hard to pinpoint.

'Oh, a bit of this and a bit of that. I waitressed when I was at … when I was younger. I know how to make a bed, and my maths skills are top-notch. I can certainly tally up a bar bill.' Her voice held a tinge of amusement. 'But like I said before, I don't have any references. I also don't have any paperwork to give you.' Her shoulders lifted in a small shrug. 'The rest of my stuff will arrive later. So I'll understand if you want to pass.'

Don looked at her for a long moment, and she held his gaze. The maritime workers that passed through the north were often itinerant and with few qualifications. Usually, it was word of mouth from skipper to skipper, and he'd only had the occasional experience with a deckhand who wanted to smoke a joint on deck at night. He didn't care what they did on land, but his boat was drug-free. Her expression was open, and her eyes clear and steady.

Even if she had no references, he had a good feeling about her, so far.

'Do you know your tax file number?'

Claire shook her head, and Don tapped a finger against his mouth and thought. 'Okay … I guess for the first trip we could pay you cash in hand. I don't usually do that, but I do need to get this sorted quickly. How would you feel about that?'

'Whatever suits you. Um, would I have to cook?'

'No. We have a chef on board.'

She nodded. 'Good. That's one thing I don't do well.'

Don narrowed his eyes. From a couple of minutes of conversation, he'd got the impression of a well-spoken, intelligent woman. It sounded like there were a few things she could do well, and again Don wondered what she was doing here in this frontier town.

She had *class.*

'Okay, have a think about it and you can let me know what you decide later today.'

Claire picked up her coffee and closed her eyes as she sipped. Her face was finely structured, and there were shadows beneath her eyes, but despite her fragility, Don sensed a quiet strength. He couldn't figure out how he knew that, but he was sure of it.

Mystery woman. The north attracted all types, many running from broken relationships. He glanced down at her fingers, but she wore no rings, and there was no tell-tale white mark on her ring finger. Although her skin was so fair, it would be hard to see.

She placed the cup carefully back onto the saucer and stood. 'I have your number. Is there a public telephone in Second Chance Bay? I don't have a mobile and there's no phone connected at the rental.'

'How about I show you?' Don grinned. 'If you can stand getting into my fish-smelling ute, I can give you a lift to the bay. You could wait hours for the taxi to come over from Karumba town. And then you still have to get the public punt across. And no, there's no phone over there.'

'The public punt?' Her forehead wrinkled in a frown.

'Yes, the punt to cross the river. That's how you get across if you don't have your own boat.'

'Oh.'

'There's no bridge. It was washed away in the wet last year, but it will take a population explosion over at the Bay for it to be replaced, and I can't see that happening this century.'

Claire looked at him carefully, without speaking, obviously weighing up the alternatives.

'Plus the chance of Joe—the taxi driver—being sober when he gets here, isn't something I'd like to put money on,' Don added with a grin. 'The call for taxis in town is minimal, and Joe's usually in the pub.

'Oh. Okay then. Thank you. I'll accept your offer.' She bent and took the handle of her suitcase before he could take it, and Don flicked a glance towards her as they walked to the ute. Her acceptance was in words only. Her body language was telling him that she didn't feel comfortable with the situation. She held her head stiffly and didn't meet his eye as he opened the door for her. Taking her suitcase from her, he swung it into the back of the ute.

Chapter 2

Claire stood on the porch of the small house and watched the sun disappear behind heavy cloud. After she'd unpacked, she sat on the soft sofa with her kindle—the only electronic device she had with her. If she didn't have a phone or a laptop, she wouldn't be tempted to look at social media—or the news. The trolls on Facebook had been cruel when the program went to air.

And for days afterwards.

Combined with the media camped outside her house, it almost did her head in. Guilt had flooded through her to think that she had been a part of that madness for a few years.

A story at any cost. Don't worry about the truth, and don't worry about who you might hurt in the process. As long as the audience numbers were there, and the ratings stayed up, the bosses were happy.

Social media was a cruel thing.

She surprised herself by falling asleep before she'd read one chapter of her book and slept soundly. The dreams that had haunted her sleep for the first couple of weeks seemed to have gone, but sometimes she had trouble remembering what had actually happened, and what she'd dreamed.

It was mid-afternoon by the time she woke, and Claire had stretched like a cat. Relaxation filled her, her limbs were loose and fluid.

Lightning flashed in the distance and it energized her. She took a deep breath; there was rain in the air. On the annual summer holiday at the farm, her grandfather had taught her how to smell rain coming, as well as the other signs that a farmer knew presaged rain. Snake tracks in the dirt meant the snakes were on the move, and rain would always follow. She looked around nervously. Snakes up here would be very different to snakes in the outback of New South Wales where Claire had researched a program. Big and venomous. The program had also looked at snakes in the tropics, and the images had stayed with her.

The house was set back from the river that she'd crossed in Don McDougal's boat this morning. The clouds had come in as she'd unpacked the few belongings from her suitcase and scoped out the house. There had been clean sheets in a linen cupboard that smelled of mothballs, and she'd made up the bed. The house was austere, but the basic necessities were there. She had somewhere to cook, sleep, eat and wash—and that was all she required.

And somewhere to hide and lick her wounds. Metaphorically,

Not with a healing tongue, but with some rational thought; this was a place to get her head together. Taking a job up here would also focus her attention away from the past few weeks, and that was a good thing.

Claire couldn't believe that she'd made such a basic mistake when she'd rented the house; there was no way to get to Second Chance Bay by road. She had assumed that there would be a bridge over the river.

All roads—all two of them from the main town of Karumba, and the road from Normanton—ended on the eastern side of the river. *That* hadn't been mentioned by the owner of the house. She'd made her enquiries, booked the house from a generic email address, and had paid six months' rent by bank cheque. There wasn't a great demand up here for rentals, and she hadn't had to supply rental references. Getting supplies in would have to be a priority tomorrow; she hadn't liked to ask Don to wait while she bought some groceries.

Claire didn't ask anyone for anything. She hadn't before, and she wasn't about to start now. She'd been let down too many times, and the last time she had been let down, it had left her life like a train wreck.

Forcing her thoughts away from her job, and her life in Sydney, she focused on the rumbling of her stomach.

The squashed muesli bar and the apple in her handbag would have to do for a meal tonight. Tomorrow she'd get herself back on the public punt and find a grocery store within walking distance. As well as food, she had to buy more hair bleach; she only had one packet left, and she didn't imagine they'd be calling into shops on the charter. It sounded like the local taxi wasn't an option. At least it wasn't far to walk from the house to the punt; Don had pointed out the jetty as they'd motored across the river.

'We can get isolated here in the wet, if the river floods.' He stood at the back of a small aluminium boat, as he steered towards the shore. His mid-brown hair was longish, and the breeze lifted it. The sun reflected off his sunglasses, but she knew that he was watching her.

Claire had perched at the front, her handbag on her lap, and her fingers gripping the handle of her suitcase. She wasn't used to boats but wasn't going to mention that, in case it jeopardised her chance at this hostess job.

If I decide I want it.

She knew her eyes were wide, but she'd have to learn how to pull herself across the river at the public crossing when she wanted to go back. How hard could it be? It was something she was going to do first up tomorrow; new experiences were ahead of her, and that would be the first. She blocked the thought of what the rest of the experiences would be; once the social media furore had settled down, she was going to have to find a new career.

Media was behind her, and she'd never go back to it.

A small boat whizzed past them and the wash rocked theirs slightly and she grabbed for her handbag as it slipped. She clung to it tightly; if she lost her bag, she'd be in all sorts of trouble; she would have to find somewhere safe in the rental to leave some of her money. It was encouraging to hear Don say it was a safe place to live.

He had said most of the locals who lived on this side of the river had their own boats. Claire knew she'd have to learn how to get across; finding another place to stay wasn't an option.

'How often does the river flood?' she asked as he'd pulled up at a small jetty; she'd told him the address she was looking for.

'This is the address you gave me. It's the Dundas house.' He pointed to the house as the motor idled. 'The last moderate flood was about ten years ago, but the biggest, the last major flood was in 74. Before I was born. Don't worry. At worst we get cut off from across town for a few days, so you always need to make sure you've got a good food store in the pantry. In the wet season that is.'

'The wet season's coming up, isn't it?'

'It is.' He looked at her curiously. 'It will start to build in six weeks or so. We've also got to watch for flooding from cyclones that can come from the west and the east. Even though we can get across to town by boat when the flow slows down, sometimes the roads from Karumba and Normanton to the south can be closed for a couple of months. How long are you staying up here? Not over the wet season?'

Claire had considered her answer carefully. She had an answer prepared for most questions, and most were far from the truth. But she had to rethink, because if there was a job going, and an ideal job on a boat far from anyone in the isolation of the Kimberley wilderness, she wanted it.

She spoke slowly. 'I guess it depends on how much work I can get up here. I may move on to Darwin in a few weeks. Or maybe not.'

Don had helped her out of the boat and carried her suitcase along the jetty. He'd waited at the gate as she'd tried the key to the rental, and she had turned with a nod when the door unlocked.

'Good to see someone here. It's been empty for a long time,' he said pointing to the north. 'Our place is another six houses along this way around the bend in the river. If you need anything this afternoon—come around. You can't miss it, there's a big white boat called *Moonshine* moored at the jetty this side of our place. Anyway, come around later, when you're settled in, and let me know if you want to talk more about the job.' He waved and began to walk back to the boat; the grass was long, and Claire had worried about snakes as she'd crossed to the gate. At least someone had mown the grass, and the gardens and lawns were neat.

Don stopped and called out to her from the end of the jetty. 'But I will need to know in the next twenty-four hours, so give it some thought. The job's yours if you want it.'

Now Claire stood watching the rain, the welcoming glow of the lights from the cottage a soft, cosy yellow behind her. But she preferred to stay out here while she decided what she was going to do. It didn't matter if she let the job on the boat pass; she had enough cash to do her for a while before she moved on again.

She let out a soft sigh. How long before she would get over what had happened, and re-enter the real world? She'd have to work again. Her parents had left her the house, but the upkeep was expensive. She had a small nest egg of savings back in the bank, but it would only last six months or so at best unless she could find a job while she decided what to do. She didn't want to rush in and sell the house as a knee-jerk reaction; it was where she'd grown up and it held too many memories to sell.

Yet.

The best decision she'd made was to come up here to the Gulf and give herself time to think. Growing up in the city, the ocean had always fascinated her, and even the smell of the salt soothed her. She had all the time in the world; she had nowhere to be, and no one was expecting her. Until she ran out of cash; this job was something she'd have to think about carefully. It all depended who was on this charter. What if they were from Sydney? Even though she'd changed her appearance, she was still recognisable. The media wouldn't be fooled by blonde hair and big glasses.

But the job on the boat was enticing; especially the thought of being paid in cash. That could extend her stay here by a few months. Claire had left her plastic cards, her social media accounts and her mobile phone in the safe at her house.

No one could find her here. Her phone and her spending couldn't be tracked.

She knew from personal experience—and was now ashamed— that she too had used those things to track someone they'd wanted to interview on the program. It wasn't hard to get the information by paying for it, even if it was a grey area of the law. Shame prickled at her neck. Getting the next story, having the biggest story had seen ethics put aside sometimes.

Maybe while she was here, she'd use this time to write an article, or maybe a book. About going off the technology grid and eschewing social media. The more she thought about the idea, the more excitement niggled at Claire; it would give her a purpose, and it would let her stay here for longer. Maybe by the time she'd done that, things would have settled down, and she would be last week's news.

When the rain stopped, she'd go around the river and see Don.

***

The rain was falling heavily when Don went outside to light the barbeque. He waited until the hotplate was smoking and then put four large pieces of marinated steak on to grill. Matt and Dane would be home soon, and it was his turn to cook. They could argue over the extra piece of steak. And they would argue. Three brothers living in a house together led to some arguments; it was just like when they'd been growing up, but at least they'd grown past wrestling on the lawn.

Poor Mum. He could still remember the day she'd put the hose on Matt and Dane when they'd been pummelling the crap out of each other after an argument about who'd caught the biggest fish.

With a wry grin, Don went back inside and brought out some sausages that had been thawing in the fridge. That was the easiest way to save an argument. But no matter what the dynamic was, theirs was a close-knit family, and he knew his brothers would lay their lives down for him if it ever came to that.

That's what came of having a liar and a gambler for a father. He pushed those thoughts away. No point dwelling on the past.

Dad had been gone for a few years now, and Mum had a happier life.

Don stood at the edge of the covered verandah watching the rain tumble down. He must have jinxed the weather by talking about rain and floods to Claire. She was a strange mix; independent and private, but with an air of fragility. As far as he'd gleaned, she was going to be living alone in the old Dunstan house. It had been empty for a couple of years since old Ma Dunstan had passed away and her grown-up kids had come up from Melbourne and tried to sell it.

Caitlin Dunstan, now obviously a mover and shaker in the Melbourne real estate world, had forgotten her Second Chance Bay roots, along with any knowledge she may have had of the real estate market—or lack thereof—in the Bay. He'd smiled when he'd overheard her telling Mum that if it didn't sell in six months, they'd Air BNB the house.

Six months later, the solid old cottage got a lick of paint, the old furniture was taken to the tip at Karumba, and some basic furniture and linen and new crockery were put in. Not surprisingly, as well as not being snapped up for sale, it also hadn't had one visitor in the eighteen months since it had been listed on the holiday site.

Until mystery woman, Claire Templeton had turned up yesterday.

But her motivation was none of his business. If she wanted the job on the *Adventurer*, it would solve his immediate problem, and she could learn as she went. He wondered who she was. Not just a beautiful woman with shaggy long blonde hair and pretty green eyes. Even though her manner had been subdued, Claire's eyes had been full of life. A couple of times he'd seen them spark, and she'd gone to say something but had thought better of it and lowered her gaze.

A mystery woman indeed.

Don was used to noisy, chattering women. His sister, Jenni, and his mother were both chatterboxes, and the house had been blissfully quiet since Jenni had married Jake, and Mum had set off on her grey nomie travels with her new partner, Rick. Don lived with his brothers, Matt and Dane in the family house where they'd grown up. He was happy there; it was a comfortable bachelor household. The football volume on the television, the dirty dishes in the sink, and the occasional line of empty beer cans along the bench on the weekend didn't bother them.

He'd thought about inviting Claire over for a barbeque, but when he'd considered the state of the house, he'd hesitated. Maybe another time; he didn't want her to think he was a slob. Not until she'd accepted the job anyway.

Despite her reticence, something had stirred inside Don as he'd looked at Claire and dropped her off at the Dunstan house.

An unfamiliar man-woman response.

A response that he'd not had since he'd had a brief fling with a backpacker he'd met in Darwin last year. He shook his head; he hadn't thought of Elke for months. It had been fun, but there'd been nothing in it, and she'd headed back to Sweden happy to finish her travels down under. If Claire was going to come and hostess on the boat, he'd make sure to keep his distance; it caused too many problems getting involved with staff, and that was a rule they'd all agreed to and stuck to firmly. Jake and Jenni had been different. Don smiled as he thought about how they'd got together when Jake had come back from Europe a couple of years ago. Sometimes when he went over to visit Jenni and Jake—they'd built an incredible tropical house on the point north of Karumba—he envied their happiness. Having a partner in life, someone to share things with would be good. Little Leni had completed their happy family; Don loved playing with her when he went over to visit between charters.

Jeez. He shook his head again before he bent down to turn down the heat on the barbeque as the meat began to sizzle, more than a little disgruntled. What was bringing on all these happy family thoughts? He couldn't ever do that; he spent too much time away to have a home base and a family who would expect him there to mow the lawn and dry the dishes.

So why couldn't he get Claire Templeton out of his head?

The front door slammed, and footsteps pounded on the timber floor down the hall that ran through the centre of the old Queenslander. The fridge door squeaked loudly as it always did, and after a couple of minutes his oldest brother, Matt, poked his head around the back door. 'Up for a beer, Donny?'

'Yep. I was waiting for you to get home. Where's Dane?'

'He's gone to the pub for dinner. He's got his eye on the new waitress.'

'Lucky her.' Don shook his head as Matt came out holding two cans of beer. He tossed one to Don. 'I knew you'd be up for a beer. It's been hot today.'

'Yeah, one of the others will warn her he's a love'em and leave'em guy,' Don said. 'He won't be late.'

'To be fair, Dane was with Nicki for a while before he lost interest.' Matt pulled out one of the wooden seats around the outside table. He shoved aside a pile of newspapers that had built up since they'd last eaten outside

'I don't think it was so much he lost interest. I think she moved on because he spends so much time away on the boats.' Don's words echoed his earlier thoughts. 'Doesn't go with happy families.'

'Jake and Jen do okay.' Matt nodded before he tipped his beer up. 'Yeah, but I get what you mean. Same goes for you too. I think you and Dane are both going to turn into cranky old bachelors.' He gestured to the untidy area around them. A couple of shovels leaned against the back wall of the house and half a dozen fishing nets stretched along between two poles. 'Two cranky old codgers living in a pig sty.'

'What about you, bro? I haven't seen you settling down.' Don pulled a face. Matt was right; it was time they had a bit of a clean-up around the place. Although they were all busy with the business, Matt had done the books and run the office for the past few years. Since Jake had come on board, and Don had branched out into his Kimberley adventure charter business, there was never enough time to do much more than sleep and eat in the family house.

'Huh, I spend all my time in the co-op trying to balance the books. All right for you two. You get to meet all the ladies out on the charters.' Matt shoulder-bumped him on the way past. 'So what's going on the barbie?'

'I pulled some marinated steaks out of the freezer.'

'Sounds good. You found a hostie, yet?'

'Maybe. I was half tempted to ask her over for dinner, but—' he gestured around the undercover barbeque area.

Matt grinned. 'She must be pretty hot to consider inviting her home. That's not like you.'

Don shook his head. 'No, she's actually a neighbour, and she doesn't know anyone in town. She only arrived here this morning. Moved into the Dunstan place around the bend, and she's looking for a job.' He frowned as the aroma of the cooking meat tickled his taste buds. 'Damn. I should have invited her.' He passed the barbeque tongs over to

Matt. 'Do me a favour. Flip those steaks over, and then clean up around here while I'm gone.'

Matt watched him with surprise as Don hurried into the house.

Chapter 3

Absorbed in her thoughts as her pen flew over the paper jotting down her ideas, Claire jumped when someone knocked loudly on the door. Apart from the occasional call of a bird, since the rain had stopped the air had been quiet and still. She stretched as she stood, and realised she was starving. Making her way to the front door, she smoothed her hands over her loose hair, still not used to having her hair out and over her face. As she passed the mirror, she glanced at her reflection. She still wasn't used to being blonde either; it was going to take some time to adjust.

Pulling the door open cautiously, she looked out onto the porch. It was still light enough to see Don McDougal standing there watching the river. The rain might have cleared away, but it had left a damp and heavy humidity behind. As she'd watched the sun set over the township on the other side of the wide river earlier, perspiration had trickled down her neck. Luckily, she'd found a small water-cooled evaporation unit—albeit old-fashioned, but still effective—in the laundry and had dragged it into the kitchen.

Don turned to her as she stepped out onto the porch.

'Hi Claire, I didn't mean to hassle you so soon.' His smile was wide, and her heart gave a big kick; the black T-shirt clung to broad shoulders and outlined strong biceps. Claire had always been a sucker for muscular arms. A reluctant grin lifted her lips. One of the half-hour programs she'd done had been in a male gym, and the team back at the station had teased her mercilessly, knowing her fascination with muscles. Back in those days, she'd shared her thoughts.

Her grin faded. And look how that had come back to bite her. Her voice was shorter than she'd intended as she stared at him. 'Hassle me?'

He folded his arms across his chest and heat warmed her cheeks as her eyes lingered on his arms and shoulders.

'I realised that you probably had no food here, and Second Chance Bay isn't the most cosmopolitan place for eating out.'

No man should fill a T-shirt so well. Or have a sexy deep voice.

Claire folded her arms as long-dormant quivers tugged at her.

'In fact, if you've had a chance to explore, you'll know there's nothing on this side of the river. It's purely residential.' He unfolded his arms and her mouth dried as her eyes came level with his chest. 'And unless you had a stack of groceries in that small suitcase, I'm guessing you haven't had dinner?'

She nodded before she could help herself, and then waved one hand. 'It's okay, I have a couple of snacks in my handbag.' She looked across at the river, now dark and swirling. 'I certainly won't be going back across the river to eat out. I'm fine. I'll go across tomorrow and get some supplies in.'

'Please come and join us. We've got a barbeque happening a couple of hundred metres away.' He lifted his head and sniffed. 'I can even smell the onions cooking from here That's how close our house is.'

'I—' Claire's mouth watered as she smelled the enticing aroma.

'Now, don't say no. There's only the two of us and we're used to cooking for five, so we have way too much food. And we'd love to have company.'

'Five?'

A wife and three children?

Before Claire could protest, he held out his arm. 'Come on. You're fine as you are, and by the way, there's no need to lock your door at Second Chance Bay.'

He stood there with his arm crooked, while Claire tried to think of an excuse, but she couldn't come up with one.

'That's very kind of you. Thank you.' She turned to the door. 'But I will get my keys and lock the door.'

When she came back out, Don was standing on the front lawn, and she was relieved when he didn't hold his arm out again.

'It's not far up to our place.'

Claire walked beside him. The grass wasn't as long as she'd thought it would be, and there was a well-worn path along the bank of the river.

'That's Jake's boat. He's my sister's husband. He moors it here because they live out on the Gulf and it's more sheltered from the weather upriver.

Claire widened her eyes as she saw the boat that Don was pointing out. The boat was a huge luxury motor cruiser and would rival any of the million-dollar boats in Sydney Harbour.

'Is your charter boat like that?' If it was, she'd give even more serious consideration to the job.

'No. *Adventurer's* a lot bigger than *Moonshine.*'

'Bigger than that?' Her eyes were wide as she stared at the million-dollar cruiser. Who were these people? Multimillion-dollar boats in a backwater in a frontier town

'Yep, but not as luxurious.' Don held out his hand as they reached the next backyard. 'There's a bit of a jump across here. We keep meaning to fill it in, but none of us ever has the time.'

Claire took his hand and his fingers were warm against hers as she jumped across the narrow ditch. She dropped his hand as soon as she was on the other side.

'She's a lot older than Jake's boat, but I've spent two years restoring her. She mightn't be as flash as some of the boats on the Kimberley waterways, but she's beautiful. A classic lady.' He held open the gate for her, but Claire hesitated.

What the hell am I doing? She'd broken the rule she'd followed for the past month. The rule that meant not getting involved with anyone. People who were going to ask questions about her.

Where do you come from? What do you do? Are you married?

But worst of all. *You look familiar. Don't I know you from somewhere?*

48

She'd changed her name. Taken off the pretentious double-barrelled Harris-Templeton when she'd left Sydney. In the media, she'd always used her second name—Sybil anyway—and along with Harris, it was a long jump to connect Sybil Harris with Claire Templeton.

Being Claire Templeton had solved a few problems; her passport and her credit cards were all under that name. Her work credit cards and her public persona had all been under Sybil Harris. For the first time, Claire wondered if she should have risked being recognised at the airport and fled overseas anyway. She closed her eyes as she remembered seeing the media circus on the news at Sydney Airport when a rumour had circulated that she was supposed to be flying to Japan. It had been news to her too; she'd been in a motel in the western suburbs of Brisbane when she'd seen the jackal media pack on the late afternoon news. They still made a story of it, even though she wasn't there, and watching them rehash the events of that night made her sick to the stomach

'Claire?'

She lifted her head as the deep sexy voice intruded on her thoughts. Don was holding the gate open waiting for her to walk through ahead of him.

'This is our place.'

Claire shook her head. 'Look I really can't intrude on your family. Your wife won't want an extra for dinner.'

The rich deep laugh sent the blood thrumming through her veins, as did his next words.

'Wife? I don't have a wife. You'll just have to put up with two blokes. Matt's my oldest brother, but we cook a good barbie between us. Plus, we'd love some company. We get a bit sick of each other, night after night. Besides as I said, it's just the two of us tonight. My other brother, Dane, has gone across to the pub for dinner apparently.' As he spoke, that familiar Aussie smell of meat and onions frying on a hotplate drifted in on the slight breeze that had come up.

She had to eat, and the thought of a barbequed meal was certainly more appealing than the apple and squashed muesli bar that were waiting in her bag. It had been kind of Don to offer; he owed her nothing unless this was his way to entice her to take the job. She'd just have to be careful with what she said. Following him through the gate, she tried to remember what she'd told him earlier.

The grass in this yard was long, and the gardens along the fence were overgrown, weeds choking the flowers that poked their colourful heads above the lush green weeds. A variety of coloured crates leaned drunkenly against a small shed, and a couple of small wooden boats were upturned on the grass. Don led her around the shed to an undercover paved area where a tall man with dark hair like his was standing beside the barbeque, a pair of tongs in one hand and an empty tray in the other. Where Don was broad-shouldered, this man was long and lean.

'Great timing,' he said with a welcoming smile. He put the plate and tongs down and held out a hand. 'I'm Matt.'

'Hello.' Claire took his hand and shook it. 'I'm Claire. It's very kind of you to feed me.' She couldn't help smiling as he laughed and gestured to Don.

'Better than looking at this boofhead all night.' He gestured around to the barbeque table. 'A boofhead who owes me, little brother. Not only did I clean up out here, but I cleared the kitchen too.'

'I hope you didn't clean up on my account,' Claire said.

'I just did as I was told.'

Don's cheeks reddened as he looked at her. 'It needed doing. Working all the time, none of us notices how we let things go.' He moved his gaze across to his brother. 'Mum and Rick are due home next week, and someone needs to weed her veggie patch and mow the lawn, or she'll be after our hides.'

'Well, it won't be me,' Matt said as he loaded the meat and onions onto the tray.

'Looks like it'll be Dane because I'll be off on a charter.' They both chuckled as Don pulled out one of the chairs at the table and gestured for Claire to sit down. 'Matt, you keep Claire entertained, and I'll get the plates and salad.'

Claire swallowed as Matt took the seat opposite her.

'So, Claire. Don says you've moved into the old Dundas place?'

She nodded.

'And you're going to work on the charters?'

This time her nod was hesitant at first. Technically it wasn't a lie if she was going to take on the job with Don. She was sick of lies these last few weeks.

The silence that followed was awkward, but Matt filled it after a minute or two. 'There's plenty of work up here. Or at least there is in the dry season. Did Don fill you in?'

'Only on the job he's got coming up.'

Matt kept talking until Don came back out with a bowl of salad on a tray with plates and cutlery. He filled her in on the boats the family-owned, and the family. Guilt and frustration settled in her chest; she hated not being able to be honest.

'That sounds good. I'm seeing as much of the country as I can.'

As Don opened the tin of beetroot that he'd brought out on the tray, Matt looked at her quizzically

'Have you been to the Gulf before?'

'No. I haven't.'

'You look familiar.' When he frowned and put his head to the side nausea clawed at Claire's stomach. She put her hand to her face to reassure herself that she was still wearing her glasses.

Oh God, not already.

Matt shrugged. 'Maybe I've seen you down in Cloncurry. Have you been there?'

Mutely she shook her head. Forcing brightness into her voice, she trotted out the words, she'd used over the last month. 'They say we all have a doppelganger, don't they?'

Matt looked over at Don and laughed.

Don shook his head, but he was smiling. 'Don't even think about it, Matthew McDougal.'

'They reckon my baby brother here, looks like that Scottish movie star. I can never remember his name, though.'

Claire looked at Don and this time she put her head to the side and couldn't help the grin tugging at her lips 'Oh yes. You could pass for Gerard Butler.'

'That's his name!' Matt slapped a hand on his thigh. 'And last New Year's Eve Mum and Jenni put him in a kilt, and the girls went wild.'

'Yeah, at least I looked better than you did.' Don's voice held a chuckle. 'Mum hired everyone's costumes online, so we weren't allowed to refuse to get dressed up.'

Claire leaned back in the chair. Now that the attention was off her, she was slowly starting to enjoy herself. She nodded as Don held up a bottle of white wine that was on the tray. 'Just half a glass, thank you.' She turned to Matt. 'Are you going to tell me who you went as?'

'All right. I'll never live it down.' He rolled his eyes. 'I was a cartoon freak when I was a kid. Mum said I was easy to look after because all I wanted to do was watch cartoons. I loved the Flintstones, so she hired me a Fred Flintstone costume.'

'That would have been cool,' Claire said.

Don's grin was wide. 'It would have been but apparently, the costume company didn't know the difference between Fred and the baby on the show.'

'Pebbles or Bamm Bamm?' Claire giggled.

'Oh, Claire. Will you marry me?" Matt put his hand on his chest. 'I've never met a girl who knew the Flintstones before.'

'That's because you go out with all the young ones. Pick someone closer to your age, and they'll know all the shows.' Don must have realised what he'd said, and Claire laughed at the horror that was on his face. 'I didn't mean you were the same age as Matt!'

'I loved my cartoons too,' she said. 'So, tell me what you wore.'

Matt looked sheepish. 'I spent the night in a green nappy thing, a girly top with bows, and a red wig with a bone through it.'

Don let out a hoot. 'And not only did he look sweet, but he also won the best-dressed at the pub for the night.'

'Yeah, and all the girls were after Gerard Butler here, and I got to dance with Mum, and all her friends who grew up with the Flintstones.'

'This was here? It sounds like it's more social than it looked when I arrived today. I only saw a caravan park and one small shop. The one where I met you, Don. I couldn't get over how deserted the streets were. The river was busier than the town.'

The joking conversation set the tone for the next hour, and Claire watched the happy banter between the two brothers as she cleared the plate of meat and salad that Don had served out for her. When she was finished, she put her cutlery neatly in the middle of the plate and stood. 'Please let me help you wash up, before I go.'

'No.' Matt waved her away. 'It's my turn and I cleaned up most of it before. I'll do it while Don sees you home.'

'I can find my own way back. I've taken up too much of your night anyway.'

'Mum taught us good manners. I'll walk you home.'

'Okay then. Thank you.' She stood, relieved that there hadn't been an inquisition. The two McDougal men had good manners.

Don stood and waited while she held out her hand to Matt.

'It was nice to meet you,' Claire said.

'And you too. I'll look forward to seeing you again.'

Claire tensed as she intercepted the look that Don shot his brother's way.

Chapter 4

Breakfast was a cup of tea, her apple and two stale biscuits that Claire found in an unopened packet of biscuits in the kitchen cupboard. The muesli bar hadn't appealed. The foray across the river to get food today would have to be her first job. Although after the fine dinner she'd been served last night, Claire wasn't hungry. Her appetite had fled a month ago, and her clothes were all a bit looser. She picked up her handbag and opened the zipper at the bottom of the bag, and pulled out a wad of cash, before peeling off two fifty-dollar notes. That should see her out for a week or two. She took half of the cash and walked around the house looking for a hiding place, but the house was so sparsely furnished there was nowhere to hide anything. Her eyes settled on the open biscuit packet sitting on the table and she pulled out the few stale biscuits and slipped a wad of notes at the end before pushing the biscuits back in and sealing the packet with a peg she'd seen beneath the kitchen sink. After putting the packet back into the bare pantry. She zipped up the concealed pocket, and put the money in her small purse, before hitching her bag onto her shoulder, and slipping on her sandals. That way if the punt sank—God forbid—or her bag was snatched, she would have half her cash left.

It was time to see if she could manage the punt to get across the river to the store. As she was locking the door a shout caught her attention.

'Claire!'

She didn't have to turn to know it was Don's voice. Biting her lip, she stood and waited as he hurried along the path. The sun was already shining out of a deep blue sky, and there was no sign of rain—or even one cloud marring the blue perfection. The river seemed to be flowing more gently this morning, and it looked bluer than it had last night. Second Chance Bay had turned out to be a very different place from what she'd expected, but she was liking it.

'Morning, Claire. I'm sorry to bother you early, but I've had someone else call about the position. Because I offered it to you first, I wanted to be fair and give you the opportunity before I talk to them.' Don's eyes were friendly, and his tone was light.

Claire took a deep breath. She'd been toing and froing all morning and had changed her mind about three times. She swallowed and held his gaze. 'No. I understand. You have a business to run.' His gaze was intent as he waited for her answer. 'If you're happy to take on a pretty raw recruit, I'd be happy to say yes.'

Don's eyes were a bright blue, fringed by dark lashes, and Claire couldn't help holding his gaze. For some reason, he fascinated her. It wasn't just the good looks, because there was no doubt he was a fine-looking man, it was more to do with his kind demeanour. His eyes held kindness and concern, and when she said yes, she was surprised to see satisfaction in them too. Deliberately she shifted her gaze back to the river; it was safer than looking into those blue eyes for any length of time.

He nodded, and she glanced at him; a satisfied smile had settled on his face.

Damn, she hoped she hadn't made the wrong decision. Life was complicated enough without a good-looking guy on the scene.

'That's great. You've saved my skin.' His face crinkled in a smile and his tone was relieved.

As her grandmother would have said, he was a gentleman. Over her years at the network, Claire hadn't encountered too many of them. She had also appreciated the obvious respect and affection between the two brothers last night. Respect wasn't something she'd seen a lot of since she'd started her career.

Before she could help herself, the words tumbled from her lips. 'Would you like to come in?' She glanced at her watch. 'A cup of tea while we talk about the job?'

'Were you on your way out?'

'I was heading across the river, but I've got all day, and nothing to do, apart from please myself.' Her voice was bright, and she was surprised how relaxed she was. She was feeling much more settled, and the bright sky and the warm breeze were adding to her serenity.

Not to mention the tall broad-shouldered man who was standing beside her.

'Thank you. It's been a while since breakfast. Dane—my other brother— had me up at some ungodly hour. He needed a hand with one of our fishing boats. I've been across the river twice already this morning. So, thanks. A cup of tea would be great.'

He followed Claire down the hall and into the kitchen, and she gestured to the small table and two chairs under the window. 'Have a seat. I'll put the jug on.' She flicked the jug on and reached down for two cups. Luckily there had been two small long-life milk in the cupboard. She bit her lip again. But no sugar.

'Um, how do you take it?'

'Black, no sugar.'

She poured the water for the tea and put the two cups onto a tray that was next to the electric jug. With a grimace, she crossed to the small pantry and took a couple of biscuits from the packet before putting it back on the shelf. A flush warmed her neck as she put some on a plate and put it on the tray. She carried the tray across to the table and sat down.

'I'm sorry. These biscuits are pretty stale. I'm looking forward to stocking the pantry.'

To his credit, Don picked up one of the gingernuts and bit into it. 'Just the way they should be. They're not teeth-breaking quality.'

Claire couldn't help the smile that crossed her face. 'I'll do some baking once I go shopping. I like to bake. My aunt gave me her old tried and true recipes.'

Where the hell had that come from? Why not tell him your life story!

Her neck heated, and she knew that the flush would have spread to her cheeks. The curse of fair skin.

'I'll look forward to it.' His voice was low, and his eyes held hers.

Claire folded her hands on the table and sat up straight. Her voice was brisk and business-like;

she could do that easily. 'What do I need to know?' She lifted her chin. 'About the position, I mean. I'll understand if you'd rather have someone experienced and prefer to go with them if that's who's enquired.'

Don shook his head. 'No. It's yours. As long as you're free from next Monday for a bit over two weeks.'

'I am. Tell me more about it. When can I see the boat? To learn my way around.'

'Not until we get over there. We leave from Wyndham. Over in Western Australia. That's where the boat is.'

Claire felt her mouth drop into a round O. 'Western Australia? I thought it was a local charter.'

He looked at her curiously. 'No, this is the Gulf, the Kimberley, and my charters are at the top of Western Australia. Does that make a difference to you?'

'Oh. I've heard of them, but I've never taken much notice of where they were. I knew it was the north.'

'Let me tell you about it, and you can decide. I keep my boat at Wyndham and that's where we pick up the passengers. They fly in from Darwin on a light plane. We offer a ten-day cruise exploring between Wyndham and the Mitchell

River, and visit King George Falls, Berkeley River and the Drysdale River and a few other well-known places.'

Claire pulled a face. 'I haven't heard of any of them.' She spoke quickly, so he didn't think she wasn't interested, because she was. 'But I'm happy to go there. I haven't seen enough of Australia.'

He looked at her curiously for a minute and Claire remembered that she'd said last night that she'd been travelling around the country.

'Up here in the north, I mean,' she added quickly.

'Well, you're in for a treat.' Don picked up the mug and sipped his tea, looking at her over the rim. 'We usually do this charter after the wet when the falls are spectacular, but we've had enough rain this winter to keep them flowing, so we scheduled an extra cruise.' A proud smile lit up his face. 'The investment in the boat has been well worth it, and the extra work I've had to put in. The demand for the cruise has been great.'

'So how do we get there? I haven't got a car.'

He waved a hand. 'Your choice. You can fly in with the rest of the crew if you want. We pay for the travel. They'll take the helicopter from Darwin but getting to Darwin from here is about three flights. Sometimes you have to go to Brisbane and back up again. Or if you're happy to take a road trip with me, I'm driving over next Monday. It'll take a couple of days to get there. I just drive and sleep and hit the road fast. I've got some gear I need to take over to the boat.' He looked sheepish. 'And I hate flying, but that's between you and me. Don't mention it in front of my brothers.'

Claire couldn't help smiling. 'I understand completely. I hate it too. And I've had enough to do me for a while. As long as you're happy for me to keep you company, I'll take the road option with you. I've got nowhere else I have to be.'

And it would save being in airports and a city for the time being.

***

Don drained the last of his tea and stood, wondering why the hell he'd felt the need to boast about the charter company. *Frig it*, he'd sounded like a sixteen-year-old trying to impress the pretty girl at school.

Claire pushed her chair back and stood. 'What else do I need to know? What do I need to bring?'

'I suppose we should talk wages and paperwork.' Don named the daily rate for the hostess position and she nodded.

'That's fine. But paperwork?' Her voice sounded nervous and she had her hands clamped together on the back of the chair. 'What sort of paperwork do you need from me? I'm travelling, and I don't have anything with me really.'

'Just the usual. Address, next of kin and all that. I need it under Work, Health and Safety rules.'

'Okay. Will I do it here or when we get on the boat?'

'You said you were going across the river for groceries?'

She nodded.

'How about I take you over now, and we can do it all at the office at the co-op? I can get you a uniform too. It's just black shorts and a white polo shirt with the logo. And a pair of white-soled shoes.'

'Okay,' she said slowly but put her hand to her lips. 'I'll come now, but shoes are a problem, I don't have any suitable for a boat.'

'What size are you.'

'A seven.'

'I'll see what Jenni can rustle up. We have a bit of stock for the crew at the office.'

'Thank you.'

Don held out his hand again. 'So we have a deal? I have a hostess?'

Claire put her hand out and he held it. The minute her fingers touched his, he wondered if he was making a big mistake. The barest touch of her

65

skin against his sent his pulse skyrocketing. She must have been aware of his reaction because she pulled her hand away, after a quick return grip, and looked at him strangely. He'd have to put a lid on this attraction; she was going to be crew. But the warm feeling stayed on his fingers as she locked the door.

Don had moored one of the family boats at the jetty near the house, and he gestured to Claire to follow him towards the house rather than to the public wharf. She hesitated when he turned left at the path, and he hurried to explain.

'We'll take my boat, rather than the public punt. I need to bring some stuff back over. And I can help you with your groceries.'

She was quiet on the way across and Don wondered if he'd upset her in some way. Maybe she didn't like him taking over.

Half a dozen local fishermen were lined up fishing near the co-op and one of them came over and caught the rope that Don threw to him and tied them off to the bollard at the end of the wharf.

'Thanks, Wattsy. Caught anything?'

'Nuh, Donny. Just a way to fill in the morning while the missus babysits the grandkids.'

He stepped out of the boat and held his hand out to Claire, but she ignored it and swung over the side to land lightly on the wharf. She still didn't speak as she followed him up to the building. Dane was out on a day charter with Jake on *Moonshine*, but Matt would be in the office. Don had to hold back his groan when they walked through the door and Jenni was at the counter.

Then he realised he was worrying over nothing. Claire was nothing more than the new hostess, and they were here to do business, and find her a uniform,

Jenni raised one eyebrow as Claire stepped into the shop behind him.

'Jen, this is Claire Templeton. Claire's here to do the paperwork to come on the *Adventurer* next week. The other hostie couldn't come.' He turned to Claire who stood quietly beside the door reading the fish species poster as though it was of great interest. 'Claire, this is my sister, Jenni.'

Claire nodded and smiled briefly, and before Jenni could start the third degree—as she always did—Don opened the door to the office. Once the door had closed, he pointed to the chair in front of the desk. 'Have a seat. I'll just pull out the employment forms.'

'It's still cash in hand, the deal?'

He lifted his head from the filing cabinet drawer to look at her when she spoke. 'Yes, just for this trip. If you work out—it was time to sound like an employer, not the adolescent lovesick goon who'd taken him over in the past few hours— 'and you stay on for more trips, we'll put you on the books then.'

Chapter 5

The hostess's job was sorted; the uniform complete with three pairs of shorts and three shirts with the Adventurer logo on them, as well as a pair of new shoes had been handed over to Claire.

'We always keep a supply on hand. Especially the shoes. The closest shoe store is down in Cloncurry,' Jenni explained as she handed over the uniform pack after Claire and Don had finished the paperwork in the office. It hadn't taken long. Claire had filled in as much of the form as she could and put Aunt Bea as her next of kin. She left her address vacant, and when Don looked at her quizzically, she made the excuse of being between apartments as she travelled. There was no need for him—or anyone—to know that she was the sole owner of a house in a leafy and well-to-do suburb on the north side of Sydney Harbour. He also looked up surprised, when she said she didn't have a mobile phone number.

Prevarication had become second nature to her, and Claire bit her lip, a little ashamed at how easy it was to avoid the truth. In contrast, she'd landed smack bang in the middle of happy family land, where no one seemed to have a cross word for anyone.

Jenni kept one eye on the cute little girl asleep in a porta cot in the corner of the store. She grabbed her brother's arm as Don went to walk over to the cot. 'Please don't wake her up, Donny. If she wakes up, that'll be the end of sleep for the rest of the day. We had a late night last night.'

'Out on the town?'

'No. Teething.'

Don grinned and hugged her as he turned away from the cot. 'The joys of being a mum, hey, little sis?'

'Yeah, and where would we go out on the town here anyway?' Jenni looked over at Claire with a smile. 'As much as I love living here, I do miss the shops and restaurants in the city. I lived in Brisbane for a few years after I finished uni.'

She looked expectantly at Claire inviting her to chat, but Claire simply nodded.

'Just as well there are no shops here. My baby sister is a shopaholic,' Don said with a grin. 'You could always get Jake to move back to Europe.'

An emphatic shake of the head. 'No. We're here to stay. This is where we want to bring our children up. And besides, there's always online shopping, Donny boy.'

Claire was made aware again of the close relationship between the McDougal siblings. A past yearning to have family close to her age flooded through her. When she was a child, she hated having no siblings. Her only cousins—and as she'd grown up, she'd discovered that Ross and Elise were very distant cousins—had lived at Gilgandra.

The McDougals were so relaxed with each other. She imagined the other brother would be much the same. Something she had little—if any—experience with. Her parents had married late in life and had been in their forties when Claire was born. Both had passed in their early seventies and the only family she had left now was Aunty Bea, her mother's younger sister.

Claire moved across towards the door, as the siblings continued to spar. When she spotted the pile of women's magazines on a table under the window, her mouth dried, and she fought to control her breathing. The panic started as a knot in her stomach and began to work its way into her chest.

Anxious to leave, to get outside, away from people, Claire dropped her head and opened the door. The sharp clang of the bell over the door made her jump and she glanced apologetically at Jenni, but the baby didn't stir.

71

'It's fine,' she said softly. 'Leni's used to that. It's only when her uncles tickle her that she wakes up.' The questions Claire had expected hadn't been forthcoming, but the calm that had filled her earlier today fled when she was in company.

How long would it take before this self-consciousness passed? Waiting for someone to say, 'Ha! I know who you are. And I know what you did. How could you be such a dreadful person?'

A shiver ran down her back, as she stood in the doorway waiting for them to stop talking. She swallowed and thought about just leaving, but her manners were better than that.

Aunty Bea had tried to talk sense into her before she'd fled Sydney. Claire had called in to see her at the aged care facility before she'd driven to Newcastle and left her car at a long-term parking station before catching the night train to Brisbane.

'Claire.' Her aunt's voice was calm, and her eyes had been sympathetic as she'd held Claire's shoulders with gentle hands. 'Stop taking it to heart so much. Everyone who knows you, and loves you, knows that you wouldn't have done it. You haven't got a calculating or nasty bone in your body.'

Claire had shaken her head. 'Aunty Bea, it was public humiliation, *national* public humiliation. I know it was a set-up, but no one else knows that and I couldn't prove it. Even when I denied knowing anything about what happened, I wasn't believed. I came out of that night's program looking like the arch bitch of television.'

'Oh, sweetie. I do worry about you. You're too soft. You've never been any good at confrontation.'

'And I trusted others to do the right thing. Just like I was brought up to do.'

Her eyes filled with tears as her aunt brushed a gentle kiss on her forehead and she was surrounded by the comforting fragrance of her familiar lavender perfume.

Now her resolve strengthened as she stepped through the door of the co-op.

Get over it. Move on. Life goes on.

***

Don was surprised when Claire walked out.

Jenni shot him a look. 'Are you sure she's hostess material? She's very quiet.'

'She'll be fine. She just couldn't get a word in with you gas bagging.'

'Good references?'

Don shrugged.

Jenni rolled her eyes. 'You mean you've hired someone without references? Again? God, Donny, when will you ever learn?'

'Keep your voice down. You might as well tell the town.' Don folded his arms and glared at Jenni. 'And you'll wake Leni up.'

'I guess it's your charter. I hope you know what you're doing.' They both turned guiltily to the door as the bell rang, but it was an older couple coming into the shop.

Don lowered his voice. 'Claire had a barbeque with Matt and I last night, and I can tell she's a good person. I have no doubt about hiring her. She's keen and she needs a job.'

'Why is she looking in Karumba? There's no work here.' Jenni whispered. 'Wait there.' She turned to serve the couple who had picked up a bag of fresh prawns from the fridge at the end of the counter. While she was serving and chatting—Don had been surprised to see Jenni there—he took the opportunity to leave.

Claire was sitting on a seat watching a ship go up river. The sun was high in the sky, and the fishing boats were coming in with the morning's catch.

'I didn't think this was an industrial port?' She turned and smiled at him, and the worry that Jenni had set churning in his gut subsided.

'It's not as busy as it used to be,' he said sitting beside her. 'The live export and the zinc have stopped now. It's just general cargo and fuel, and fishing products for export.'

'Different to what I expected. Anyway, thanks for the uniform and everything. I'll go and do my shopping now, and I'll see you next Monday,' she said.

Don frowned. 'I'll give you a lift to the town, and then I'll take you back across the river.

She shook her head. 'There's no need. I can manage.'

'Look, I've got nothing on until this afternoon when Dane and Matt come in on the charter. I'm at a loose end, and it's crazy for you to take the punt.'

She lifted her head and stared at him, and he could almost see the wheels turning in her head.

'I'm not your boss yet. Just a friend offering to help out. And while we're there I can get some stuff for when we're travelling across to Wyndham next week.'

The smile that slowly lifted her lips was sweet. Her face lightened, and her eyes crinkled at the edges. 'In that case, I guess I have to accept.'

'I leave my ute parked in the shed behind the co-op. I'll go and get it. He gestured to the road. 'I'll meet you over there on the corner.'

By the time Don reached the shed and turned around Claire was standing on the corner. A slight breeze was blowing in from the Gulf, and her hair ruffled in the breeze. As she reached up to push it back from her eyes, her dress hugged her soft curves and she smiled at him again. He wondered if she realised how that gentle smile transformed her cool face into something softer. More approachable. He turned away, cursing himself for being attracted to her.

He had a two-thousand-kilometre road trip ahead in her company, not to mention ten days on the boat.

***

It was a couple of kilometres around to the main town, and Claire looked at the landscape with interest. Everything was so flat here; along the side of the main road, large birds stood in the water that filled the channel along the edge of the flat paddocks, poking their bills in and out of the water searching for food. The IGA was in a short street with only a few shops. A bank, a real estate agent and a takeaway store completed the row of old buildings. A store with bakery on the sign was closed and, as she looked closer, the windows were boarded up.

Don followed her gaze as she parked the car. 'We've had a few shops close here as the population has decreased since the zinc mine closed. Bread and the newspapers are brought up from Normanton every day now.'

He came around and opened the door of the ute for her. Claire held her handbag tightly as she climbed out, thinking about what she had to buy.

At the front of the shop, four elderly men sat in a line on the bench beneath the window.

'Papers not in yet, Harry?' Don called as they approached.

'Nah, the bugger's late again. He'd better get here, it's past cuppa time.' Harry—Claire assumed he was the one who answered—looked at her curiously as she followed Don into the store. Heat ran up her neck as his next words followed them in.

''Bout time that McDougal lad got himself a woman.'

'She's a looker too. Bit skinny on it, though,' came the reply, followed by a hacking cough.

Don stopped near the grocery trolleys and shook his head. 'Sorry a few old locals with no manners.'

She reached up and swapped her sunglasses for the spectacles she'd pulled from her bag. 'It's okay. I'm used to all types.' Claire reached for a second trolley, ignoring the stand of glossy gossip magazines beside the cash register that made her stomach plummet to her feet. At least she wasn't on the covers anymore. Self-consciously, she reached up and touched her hair, reassuring herself that she wasn't recognisable. 'So, tell me. What will I need to take in the way of food on the road trip? Will we eat at the motels, or eat as we travel?'

'Ah.' This time there was a dull flush on Don's cheeks. 'I should have explained the trip a bit better. There are no motels. We go bush along the Savannah Way.'

'Go bush?' Her voice caught in a gulp.

'Yeah, we'll be swagging it, and cooking for ourselves. Don't worry about food for the trip. You just get whatever food you need for the house, and the personal stuff you need for a few weeks, and I'll sort the rest.'

Chapter 6

Don *had* sorted the trip well. Just after dawn, four days later, they crossed the river in his boat to where his ute was parked at the co-op. Claire's suitcase was packed with her new uniform, her shoes and some of her clothes—and two bottles of hair bleach for touching up the regrowth.

With Don ferrying her across the river, she hadn't had to face the public punt, but it was something she had to learn to do on their return.

Nerves had skittered in her tummy all night, and she wondered if she was doing the right thing, or if she'd just jumped at a chance to get further away. She couldn't hide forever; eventually, she'd have to resurface. There'd be media interest when they found her, but she knew how the news worked. By that time—a few months after the event, she'd be the mystery woman who had reappeared and the focus in the media would have changed.

Claire well knew how fickle the media game was. Always chasing the next big story, the highest ratings, the most viewers. And it didn't matter who got trampled in the process. Now that she was on the other side, it was so much easier to see what a sham it was.

How naive was I to think I could make a difference to the world?

Her eyes were gritty when her alarm trilled at four a.m., and she'd stumbled into the bathroom, her head aching. Splashing water on her face she tried to wake up and dispel the awful dull feeling that had stayed with her as she'd thought of the past few months.

Of course, Don had arrived early; when she'd heard the boat revving at the jetty outside the back of the house Claire had her head in the laundry tub washing her hair after touching up the regrowth again. If she'd known how hard it was to keep her hair blonde, she would have reconsidered dyeing it in Brisbane. But she hadn't been thinking straight then, and she was getting quite used to the ash-blonde colour. She hurried from the bathroom before he reached the front door, rubbing at her eyes. They were stinging from where the hair bleach had splashed up from the small sink.

Damn.

'You there, Claire?' His voice preceded a knock on the door.

'Won't be long. My bag's just inside the door. It's unlocked.' She wiped her eyes and switched on the hair dryer and quickly dried her hair before plumping it up with her fingers.

Excited anticipation warred with the nerves in her stomach. A quick coffee and a Panadol had chased the headache away. She'd only seen Don once since he'd helped her carry her shopping a few days ago. He'd called in one evening as she'd been cooking biscuits to take on the trip to tell her when they would be leaving.

She hadn't invited him in, but his nose had twitched as the smell of baking wafted from the kitchen.

'That smells good.'

Heat had run up her neck. 'I thought I'd do some baking to take while we're travelling. Nothing like a bikkie to go with a cuppa,' she said self-consciously. She didn't want him to think she was trying to score points or anything.

After three nights on her own with no computer or phone, and no one to talk to, boredom had come screaming in, and she was thankful she had the road trip and the charter to look forward to. She'd walked along the river to the south, keeping an eye out for snakes—and other residents—but hadn't seen either. The punt was an intricate-looking arrangement of ropes and pulleys, and her stomach sank as she contemplated having to do that in the future.

What an isolated place.

'Well, that's what you wanted,' she'd muttered to herself as she walked along the mudflats to the south of the punt jetty. A variety of birdlife scurried ahead of her and crabs skittered across the wet mud at the edge of the water.

It was peaceful, and she could feel herself healing. The upside was that calm had settled, and the fear of being recognised hadn't been a problem that was constantly with her. The other benefit was that she'd used the time to get some more words down, and that kept her grounded. She was rested and looking forward to something different.

The adrenaline-fuelled rush to get here had kept her hyped, but now she was settled, Claire wondered what she was going to do with her time when she was here in the house. There were only so many walks she could take before the river closed into thick bush at the south. She hadn't gone the other way as there were more houses to the north. And if she was honest, she didn't want Don to think she had gone looking for him. It must be the state of mind she was in; she'd never been attracted to someone so fast.

She jerked her thoughts back to the present and yawned as she hurried to the small living room. The door was open, and her suitcase was gone. 'I'll just get the stuff out of the kitchen,' she called as

Don came back to the door. She hadn't been sure what to wear, so had opted for a pair of long cargo pants, a T-shirt, and the sturdy walking shoes she'd brought from Sydney. She'd thrown them in at the last minute, unsure of what she'd need in the wild north. She certainly hadn't expected a two-thousand-kilometre road trip, sleeping under the stars in a swag.

With a rugged sea captain. A good-looking one. Not to mention one that oozed sex appeal.

'All ready?'

Claire nodded as she walked to the door, a Tupperware container full of assorted homemade biscuits in one hand and her handbag gripped firmly in the other. She'd worried too much about leaving money in the house while she was gone, so last night she'd shoved the notes into her handbag and zipped up the compartment. Hopefully, there'd be a safe or somewhere secure on the boat to put her bag while they were on the charter.

'You look the part.' Don looked at her and there was a touch of admiration in his eyes.

'I hope I don't let you down.' She was nervous about camping out. There weren't going to be many places for rest stops on the road. The day he'd come to see her, Don had dropped in a book, and a brochure for the charter and she'd read them with interest.

There were two ways to go west and he'd chosen the shortest, but the downside as the book told her, was that it was a very rugged road. She'd felt like she was doing research for a program as she'd read the book. The Savannah Way was classed as an adventure drive and started in Cairns in the east and went through the savannahs of the Top End—thus the name, she thought with a grin—before ending at Broome in the west.

The photographs of gorges, rivers and waterfalls had piqued her interest. Then when she'd turned to the brochure her excitement had grown, pushing away further the dark thoughts that had dogged her for the last month.

'You'll be fine. Even though we're going to do it fast, you'll get to see a part of the country that few people see.'

Claire locked the door behind her, checked that her handbag was securely on her shoulder and looked up at him with a smile.

'Lead on, McDuff.'

'That's McDougal.' Don grinned back at her before he turned away to the jetty. As she followed him, Claire let her gaze wander over the broad shoulders and the snug-fitting jeans.

As they crossed the river, she focused on keeping her gaze on the mangroves along the north side past the houses. She pretended to be watching the pair of jabirus that were standing in the shallows.

This attraction to Don was something she was going to have to be very aware of. Careful that he didn't see her looking at him or daydreaming about him holding her.

She was here to work for him, and he was her boss. And she certainly didn't want any more complications in her life. She'd had enough already to do her a lifetime.

***

Don was carrying spare fuel, but he still stopped at Normanton to top up before they turned onto the Savannah Way.

'Every little bit counts when there's a long way between fuel stops.' He glanced across at Claire as they turned into the service station. 'Do you want to grab a coffee while we're here? This will be the last chance for real coffee until we reach Katherine the day after tomorrow.'

She shook her head. 'No, I'm fine, but I might just use the amenities.'

She slipped out of the car, those crazy large sunglasses covering half her face, the handbag that she always held close tightly beneath her arm and walked quickly across to the ladies' room that was separate from the service station main building. By the time, he'd filled the ute and paid for the fuel, she was back in the passenger seat, sitting low in the seat.

Don started the car, wondering for the umpteenth time what her story was. On the way down to Normanton, they'd chatted—or rather he'd talked, and Claire had uttered the occasional yes or no in response to any questions he'd asked her. He was careful not to get personal; it was very clear that she wasn't prepared to share anything. All he knew was that she was from Sydney and that she had a recipe book from her aunt.

But her life—and her problems—were none of his business.

He had a hostess for the charter; he had someone to talk to on the bloody long trip across to Wyndham, and an added bonus was that she was damn fine to look at.

Jeez, how sexist did that sound, he thought. Jenni and Mum would be right onto him for thinking that.

But hell, he was a red-blooded male, and of course he appreciated a fine female figure. There was nothing wrong with admiring from afar; he knew how to keep his distance and he didn't want to spook her.

From Claire's point of view, she was heading into the unknown, with a stranger she hadn't met a week ago, to a job that she hadn't even heard about a week ago, to a place she hadn't heard of.

If it had been his sister doing that, he would have told her she was foolish, but he sensed that foolish wasn't a word that applied to Claire Templeton.

'Would you like me to share the driving if you want a break?' Her quiet voice interrupted his thoughts as they turned off the bitumen onto the iconic road known as the Savannah Way. She rushed on. 'I know you wouldn't have anyone to share the driving if I hadn't come with you, but I'm happy to take a turn.'

Don nodded. 'I'd appreciate that. It'll get us there a bit faster if I can snooze in the car. We can drive later in the day.' He nodded ahead. 'We've got two hundred ks of dirt ahead, but once we get to the Gregory Downs turnoff, the road's sealed all the way to Burketown and you can take over. You'll just have to keep an eye out for road trains because it's only a single-lane road.'

'I'm pleased you'll let me help.' Claire turned from the window. 'And you don't have to worry, I learned to drive on dirt roads in the outback.'

He nodded again, reluctant to ask any questions. Her privacy was something she hung onto like that damned handbag.

"Can I ask you something, Don?'

He changed back a gear as the road narrowed, and the ute juddered on the patch of corrugations. Dust billowed behind them, but he kept an eye ahead for anything coming towards them as the road levelled out again.

'Sure, what's up?' he said.

'You said you leave the boat over there. How come you live so far away?'

He shrugged. 'I ask myself the same question every time I do this trip, over and back. I'm going to have to seriously consider living over there.'

'Where's over there?'

'Probably Wyndham. But it's a small place. And I guess if I'm truthful—' he cleared his throat, thinking he was going to sound like a wuss.

'If you're truthful?' she prompted.

'I'd miss the family too much. Don't get me wrong, I'm not a sensitive new age man or whatever the current term is. As much as we blue a lot of the time, I enjoy my brothers' company. And I am a quarter-owner of the company there, so I should be there to help.' He was thoughtful as he stared ahead for a few minutes before he glanced across at

Claire. 'I'm thirty-two and except for when I did my marine courses in Tassie, I've never lived away from Second Chance Bay. I guess that makes me sound pretty boring.'

Claire shook her head. 'No. Not at all. I think you're very lucky. If I'm truthful—'

Don eased back on the accelerator a bit, so he could hear her quiet words over the roar of the engine.

'Yes?' It was his turn to prompt.

'If I'm truthful, I'm envious of your family life. I've only met your brother and sister, but I've heard the way you speak of your mum and your other brother and it's obvious that you all have a good relationship.'

'It wasn't always like that. Pardon my language, but our dad was a real bastard. I think since he died, we've all got a lot closer.' Don stared ahead and was surprised when Claire reached out and lightly touched his hand on the steering wheel. Her touch prompted him to put into words what he was thinking. 'I've always worried that his traits might have passed onto me. That's why I've never settled down with anyone.'

'Trust me, you have nothing to be ashamed of or embarrassed about. These days, you don't come across many people who care about others like that.' Her voice was tight, and her tone was cynical. 'You're a good person, Don. I can tell that.'

The more he got to know her, the more certain he was becoming that Claire was running away from someone.

An abusive partner?

It wasn't any of his business. He'd looked at her employee form, and it had the name of a person with the address of an aged care facility as the next of kin. He hadn't commented when he'd seen the bottles of hair bleach she'd bought, but as he thought more about it, he knew she was hiding from her past. His hand clenched on the steering wheel.

If someone had tried to hurt her, they deserved a thrashing themselves. He couldn't help the question that spilled from his lips. 'Do you have family back home?'

He glanced across and he regretted asking as her hesitation became obvious. Her hands gripped the bag tightly, and eventually, she looked up at him just before he turned his attention back to the road.

'I only have my aunt. Aunt Bea, the one on my employment form.' She took a deep breath. 'She and Uncle Jack were out on a farm at Gilgandra, and I spent a lot of time out there when I was growing up. I've got a couple of cousins somewhere—and their kids— but I haven't seen them for a long time. Seeing you with your brother and sister brought home to me how much I missed out on not having a family. I'm an only child; the only company I had growing up was imaginary.'

He kept his voice light and tried not to sound like he was digging. 'One day, you'll settle down and you can create your own family.'

'Maybe one day.' Her voice was wistful, rather than sad. 'The biological clock is ticking faster every day.'

'If it's not a rude question, how old are you?'

'Same as you. Thirty-two.'

Don was surprised; she looked much younger than he did, but before he could answer his attention was drawn to the road ahead. A huge cloud of red dust ahead indicated a large vehicle was approaching.

He looked to each side of the road; there was a flat piece of cleared ground in the scrubby bush that had obviously been used as a campsite as wheel tracks went into it. He wrenched the wheel to the left and accelerated up the slight incline to the flat.

'Road train,' he said as they headed bush.

Claire turned around and looked through the window behind them. 'Holy shit!'

Don grinned as he did a three-point turn so they could go back onto the road. Red dust filled the air around them, and the smell of cattle on the truck pervaded the interior of the ute even though the windows were up and the air conditioning was on.

She shook her head as he backed up. 'That's a road train? I didn't like to show my ignorance. How long was that?'

Don looked down the road before he turned back onto the dirt. The back of the long high vehicle was disappearing down the road towards Normanton. 'Anywhere between forty and fifty metres long.' He grinned. 'Do you still want to share the driving?'

Claire let go of the bag and folded her arms. 'Give me some time to get over that awful smell and I'll think about it. What on earth is it? It smells like something died.'

'Cattle.' He looked at her curiously. 'You've never seen a road train hauling cattle before?'

Her eyes were sparkling now. 'No. You don't see that in the city at all.'

They set off along the road again, but the serious conversation had been interrupted by the road train. But as Claire looked out the window watching the landscape go by, Don felt as though he had got to know her a little more.

He reached down and turned the stereo on.

'If you don't like the music, just let me know. I'm a Johnny Cash fan. My family pays out on me.'

As the first song came on, she turned, and her smile was sweet. 'Love that song. Johnny Cash is one of my favourites, ever since I saw the movie about his life.'

A warm feeling settled in Don's chest as they headed west.

Chapter 7

As it turned out, Claire didn't drive that day. She was fascinated by the small settlements they drove through; it was a whole new world, nothing like the idealised outback she'd seen in the movies. Doomadgee was red dust and abandoned cars; small groups of aboriginal people stood looking curiously as they drove through.

So different to the city, Claire realised what a narrow existence she'd led; she had travelled widely overseas and had visited a few Australian cities with the program, but she'd never experienced anything like this remote country before.

'I guess I'm seeing the true outback,' she commented as they approached a wide river ahead,

'You are.' Don threw a quick glance her way. 'It can be a bit confronting at times. Wait until we get to Katherine.'

'It makes me feel as though I don't know my country at all.'

'You've never been north before?'

'Or to the outback.' She shook her head. 'No further west than Gilgandra, or north of Brisbane. I went there for a conference once, so I didn't see too much of the city anyway.'

She could have kicked herself when Don replied with a question in his voice. 'A conference? That would be a new world to me. I've never been to one.'

'Pretty boring.' She injected disinterest into her tone. 'You haven't missed much.' She wished she hadn't mentioned Brisbane as the memories came flooding back. That had been the conference where they'd picked up the lead to the story that had eventually been her downfall.

It had also been at that conference that she'd first shared a bed with Ben, the program director. They'd been out for dinner a few times, and he'd been persistent about taking the relationship further. It had taken a while before she'd agreed to go out with him in the first place.

'No, Ben. We work together. Social life and work don't mix.'

He'd laughed and told her she was old-fashioned. 'This is the twenty-first century, babe.'

Maybe she was old-fashioned. Maybe she'd chosen the wrong profession.

No. Claire bit her lip as the ute slewed to the left in some loose sand; she had made a poor choice.

In her career, and in sleeping with Ben. It was all linked, and she hadn't realised and look where she had ended up now. But if old-fashioned meant caring about people's feelings, and not wanting to be in the limelight, that's the way she'd rather be.

Strangely for the sort of job she had, Claire had hated being in the limelight. She'd seen her role as a different way of promoting social justice; it was why she'd studied law. The job had been everything she'd wanted to start with, until the change of management last year. Ratings had always been important, but their reporting had held integrity before then. The show had won awards and they had been ethical.

Until the management change, ratings and advertising dollars took precedence over truth.

And then the program aired the week after she'd slept with Ben. Her world had come crashing down.

'Bulldust.'

'What?' Claire jumped and stared at Don with a frown, worrying for a moment that she'd spoken her thoughts out loud.

'That was a bull dust hole we just hit.' His frown matched hers. 'The road's worse than I thought it would be; we're going to have a slower trip than I hoped for. There's been a lot of cattle moved out here.'

She must have looked confused.

'Road trains,' he explained. 'They chop the road up and the bull dust can settle into holes. You never know what's under the dust until you go down into one. I'll drive for the rest of today. I was going to try to get to Borroloola for tonight but that's still three hundred ks away. We'll have to camp at the Robinson River crossing instead.'

'Whatever you say, boss. I'm just following along.' She smiled. Even though she was feeling low, the conversation had pulled her out of those thoughts that sent her into a downward spiral.

'The next couple of days will be quicker. This is the only unsealed part of the road.'

'I'm in your hands.' Heat rushed up Claire's neck when he glanced over at her. The silence was heavy. After a moment, Don reached over and turned the stereo back on.

Claire turned back to the window, lost in her thoughts. But this time it wasn't about work.

Don McDougal was hard not to think about.

***

The road was the worst that Don had seen it, in the half a dozen trips he'd done in the past year. Road trains loaded with cattle, and numerous grey nomies travelling the Savannah Way in the dry season had brought the road into a shocking state. He tried to hide his displeasure; the last thing Claire needed was a grumpy boss and a driver she had to spend the next two days and nights with. They'd stopped for a quick cuppa out of the thermos he'd brought, and he smiled when Claire had held out the Tupperware container.

'A melting moment or an ANZAC bikkie?'

He'd had two of the freshly baked biscuits, and then another two when they'd stopped for the sandwiches he'd packed early that morning.

The consolation was that once they reached Borroloola, the road was tarred; narrow but without the worry of washouts and bull dust. It made the thought of moving to Wyndham and basing himself on the boat between charters much more attractive. If the road stayed in this condition, he'd either have to consider going the long way across the Barkly Highway each trip or relocating.

So, if he moved, he'd be there by himself. It was time he was independent. Jake had lived in Europe for ten years and it hadn't killed him. Being on the boat all the time and not travelling back and forward would give him more time to keep it in top condition. And more importantly, more time to focus on getting a permanent crew, and not go through the dramas of getting deckhands, a chef and a hostess every trip. Matt and Dane would have to cope without him running the fishing charters.

How sad had he sounded when he and Claire had shared some stories? He was bloody thirty-two years old, and he'd made it sound as though he couldn't survive without his family close by.

Hell, the way she'd shared her childhood with him, she'd done that for most of her life.

So as soon as this charter was over, a move to Wyndham and living on the boat was a priority. He wouldn't have to face this treacherous road again. As he planned the year ahead in his mind, he took his attention from the road for a split second.

The steering wheel wrenched to the left and he had to grip it tightly as the ute tipped into a large hole on the left side.

Claire screamed, and she bounced forward, her head almost hitting the windscreen, but her seat belt held her tight.

'Bloody hell!' Don held on for grim death as the ute tried to roll over to the passenger side. A loud clunk came from the suspension as something let go, and the vehicle sagged to the other side. The motor screamed, and he knocked it out of gear and lifted his foot from the accelerator, but the motor kept whining as it sunk into the deep hole. He killed the ignition and turned to Claire.

'Are you okay? Did you hit your head?'

'No, I'm fine. I just got a fright. What happened?'

She looked up at him from the passenger side, and Don realised how deep the ute had sunk on that side.

'More bull dust. If I'd known the road was this bad, I wouldn't have come along the Savannah Way.' Don pushed open the driver's door and the ute creaked and rocked as he moved to get out.

Claire's eyes widened, and she reached down for her handbag that had ended up on the floor. 'Should I get out too?'

'Just stay there until I suss out the damage. There's no danger. We're not going to roll now.'

'But we could have?' Her voice trembled, and Don felt bad.

He reached over and put his hand on her arm. 'It's okay. I might have to change a tyre and then we can find somewhere to camp for the night and get an early start tomorrow.'

He walked around to the passenger door and held it open while Claire climbed out. The ute was at a precarious angle and some of the load in the back had shifted. Luckily he'd tied the jerry cans of fuel and water on securely, and they were still firm against the backboard.

'What can I do to help?' she asked. He glanced up from where he had squatted at the back of the ute.

'Just wait there for a sec. I'm going to have to get the ute out of the hole, and then try to find somewhere to set up camp.' He stood and put his hands to his eyes. The sun was dipping below the row of paperbarks ahead, and he realised that they weren't far from the river crossing. He climbed back into the car and called out. 'Just wait over near that cleared patch.'

She stood back as he'd directed, and Don started the car and put it into low range. He backed it up as far as he could and then put the accelerator down, and the ute rocked from side to side as he cleared the hole. He drove down the road about fifty metres and then climbed out. He beckoned to Claire and hid a smile as she walked gingerly down the road, her eyes on the fine red dust in front of her. By the time she reached him, he had squatted in front of the front left tyre.

Her once clean shoes were red with dust, and he smiled as she bent and unrolled the bottom of the cargo pants and a puff of fine dust dropped to her shoes.

'Welcome to the Top End,' he said.

'Hmm. Are the Kimberleys like this?'

'Even better. There's still red dirt, but it's broken by spectacular gorges and waterfalls. Wait till we get to the Cockburn Ranges and you see the western face lit up in a red glow at sunset. It's a magnificent sandstone escarpment that rises high above the surrounding plains. There's black siltstone embedded in the sandstone and the stripe goes for hundreds of kilometres.' He stood and shook his head with a rueful grin. 'Listen to me! I've been practising my patter for the boat too much. I sound like a bloody tourist brochure.'

Claire held his gaze and he found it hard to look away. 'You make it sound beautiful.'

'It is a beautiful part of the world. That's why tourists pay ten thousand dollars a trip to see it.'

'I noticed on the brochure it's classed as a luxury holiday.' Her hands clenched nervously, and she bit her bottom lip. He'd noticed her do that a few times when she was out of her comfort zone. 'Where do most of the guests come from?'

'Mainly from the city. Sydney. Melbourne, Adelaide, and often from overseas.'

'Oh.'

Claire dropped her gaze and scuffed the ground with her boot.

'Well, the tyre's okay, and I can't see anything wrong with the suspension, so we'll head down the road away. The campsite's not far away.'

Chapter 8

Two hours later they'd made a camp on a flat clearing a couple of hundred metres from the road. Don set up the swags and got a fire going, while Claire got the eskies and set up a small camp table and two camp chairs that were on the back of the ute.

She stood back and took a deep breath as contentment filled her. The occasional car went past—but no more road trains, thank goodness— and no one else had camped near them. Lights flickered upriver a couple of kilometres, and on the far horizon, a bright light lit up part of the night sky.

'That's the aboriginal settlement over at Robinson River,' Don explained as Claire stared at the light in the distance.

Claire looked around nervously. The firelight lit up the centre of the camp, and Don had lit a camp light on the table, but dark shadows encroached on the edges of the camp, and the occasional rustle and crack came from the scrubby bush. She had put her handbag in the swag and zipped up the canvas.

'Is it safe to camp here?'

'Yes, it's all safe here. No one will bother us. If we were in Borroloola, we'd probably set up camp in a locked compound. There's a serious alcohol problem there that the community is working hard to control.'

She shook her head. 'No. I meant the wildlife, not people.'

As Don had set up the camp, she'd asked if they could camp closer to the river, and he'd led her over to a sign at the side of the road.

'Crocodiles inhabit this area. Attacks cause injury or death,' she'd read aloud. She jumped back as though they were going to come up the hill where the road went into the river. 'Crocodiles?' she squeaked. 'Here? We're way inland!'

'They're here. They follow the major rivers and floodplain billabongs into freshwater rivers, creeks and swamps, so we always have to be careful.'

Claire had backed away from the sign a few more steps and pointed to the swag. 'And you expect me to sleep in a tent on the ground where crocodiles roam?'

Don chuckled, and her temper burred.

'Don't laugh at me. I'm serious. Are there crocodiles where you take the charter?'

This time he looked sheepish. 'Yes, but mostly freshwater. They'll bite if you step on them, but they won't kill.'

'Great,' she muttered. 'That's okay then, what's a bite between friends.'

She'd followed Don back to the camp and stood by him as he put the barbeque plate on the fire. Once the meat was sizzling, she went over and picked up one of the camp chairs and put it in the light of the fire. Don sent her a curious glance and she pulled a face at him.

'At least I can see around me if I sit near the fire. Do you have a doctor or a nurse on this boat of yours?'

'There's no need. Most of the staff have emergency care and CPR. I noticed you did on your employee from.'

'I do, but I don't know that it extends to crocodile bites. You'd probably need more than a band-aid,' she said drily.

'I like this feisty Claire.' Don put the tongs on the table and headed across to the esky. 'I was starting to think you were regretting accepting the job.'

'Only in some ways,' she said slowly.

'Would you like a beer or a wine or a soft drink?'

'A cold beer would be great, thanks.' Claire watched the flames as they subsided into the coals. Shades of blue, yellow and magenta contrasted with the orange glow of the embers. She nodded her thanks as Don passed the cold can to her and pulled up the other chair near the fire.

'Penny for them?' he said softly.

***

Don settled back into the canvas chair and sipped at his beer, the cold a welcome relief to his parched throat. Red dust had surrounded them today, and the camping gear was covered in a fine film of red. He waited for Claire to reply, and for a while, he thought he might have overstepped the mark. She'd been much more relaxed this evening, joking about crocodiles and band-aids; He'd seen that spark in her personality that he'd suspected was underneath her cool exterior.

'Are you worried about the charter?'

When she lifted her head, the sadness in her eyes surprised him. 'Yes.'

He cleared his throat and pulled his chair closer. 'Look, I didn't want to cause you any worry, talking rot about crocodiles and stuff. I was teasing. We might see the occasional freshie, but we only swim where it's safe. Please don't worry.'

She lifted the can, and he watched as she closed her eyes and sipped. The silence was long.

Her voice was bleak when she finally spoke. 'I have a big favour to ask you. I'm sorry I can't tell you why, but I need to ask you something.'

'Okay.' His voice was wary. He didn't want to promise anything, but he'd consider whatever she asked.

'If anyone on board thinks they know me, would you tell a little white lie for me? Say I've been in the north for a few months. Only if they ask, that is.' Her voice rushed on quickly. It seemed as though once she'd started, she couldn't stop. 'Don't worry, I'm not a criminal or anything. I haven't broken the law.' Her laugh was bitter as she lifted her head and her eyes held his. 'That's quite rich, isn't it? I'm actually a lawyer.'

This time his eyes narrowed. 'A lawyer?'

Claire nodded, and he couldn't look away as the tip of her tongue appeared and she ran it over her top lip. 'Yes, a lawyer,' she finally replied. 'I went to university straight out of school. Please just trust me when I say I have done nothing wrong. I just found myself in a situation where I was accused of something.' She waved one hand and her beer tipped over in her lap. 'Oh damn.' She jumped up and put the can onto the table and dabbed at her cargo pants with the bottom of her T-shirt. Don walked over to the ute and brought back a roll of paper towels.

'Here you go. Use this.'

'I'll smell like a brewery now.'

'At least it's better than a cattle truck.'

That got a quiet laugh from her. 'Please trust me when I say I'm not in the wrong. I'm just taking some time out. Lying low from the media and thinking about what I want to do with my life.'

'If the situation calls for it, I don't have a problem saying you've been up here for a while.'

'Thank you.'

He let it go at that as he turned to the barbeque. 'Time to eat, hey? How hungry are you?'

'Surprisingly, very hungry. I shouldn't be, I've barely used up any energy sitting in a car all day!'

'It's the fresh country air that does it, and anything cooked over a fire is always more appealing too.'

'Thank you.' Claire nodded as he handed her a plate piled high with steak and onions.

'There's some bread rolls in the esky if you want to make a burger?'

She shook her head, her mouth already full as she tucked in.

As they sat around the fire, the mood was relaxed. The tension had eased from her shoulders, and Don was able to get a laugh a few times as he told her anecdotes about the north.

The more she laughed, the more he dug deep for stories. 'You'll probably meet ol' Cruzer if you stay in the Dunstan house for a while. He'll come knocking on your door.'

'Ol Cruzer?' Claire leaned back in the chair, one hand on her lap, and the other relaxed by her side.

'Yeah, he's an old fella who claims he was shipwrecked in the Gulf back in the sixties. He gets around in tattered old pants, no shirt and I don't think he owns a pair of shoes. He's harmless, but once he hears you're there, he'll come to visit, and bring you some of his speciality.'

'Fish?'

Don laughed. 'No.'

'Prawns?'

'No.' He watched her as he put one finger to her lip and her eyes lit up.

'I give up.'

'Honey.'

'That's kind of him.'

'It is,' Don chuckled.' But you have to be careful not to spread it too thickly on your toast. 'Ol Cruz grows some "special" green plants out in the bush, and his bees live around the flowers. It's known locally as Happy Honey. Just a local myth, I don't think it could be true.'

Claire was still laughing as they stood and cleared away the dishes.

'I'll go down to the river and wash them.' Don gathered the dishes into a small plastic crate

'The river?' Her laughter died.

'Don't worry. I'm not going to do a Crocodile Dundee. I'll just fill the tub and come back up here.'

He looked down as Claire reached out and held his arm. A tingle ran up his forearm. 'Are you sure it's safe? Do you want me to come with you?'

Don went to say no but then thought twice. 'If you want to. Two pairs of eyes are better than one.' He regretted saying that a few minutes later as he stood at the edge of the river and shone his flashlight around. He reached back and handed it to Claire who was standing at a respectable distance from the water.

He lowered the crate and it was almost full when the light flashed past him and hovered in the middle of the river.

'What's that?' Claire's voice was tight.

Don stood and lifted the crate, some of the water sloshing on his arms. He followed the direction of the beam where two red glowing eyes were highlighted in the middle of the river. 'Hmm, well that would be a crocodile.'

'Really.' This time it was a squeal that came from behind him.

'Yep.'

Claire shone the flashlight along the bank and her sigh of relief was loud. 'There's none on the shore.'

'No, and he won't bother us either. Come on, let's get back to the camp.'

As Don washed the dishes, Claire dried and repacked them.

'They won't come up here, will they?' She looked around nervously. 'Should we sleep in the ute?

'No.' Don hastened to reassure her. 'It's safe. We're far enough away.'

Claire didn't look convinced as she headed to the swag. 'Good night.'

'Sleep well,' he said. 'We've got a long day tomorrow.'

##

Don sat by the fire until the coals had burned to nothing. He kicked some dust over the embers and made sure that the fire was out. He left the side of this swag closest to the ute unzipped. It wasn't crocodiles that you had to watch for out here in the Savannah wilds. It wasn't unknown to have unwelcome visitors of the human variety sniffing around a vehicle in the middle of the night.

Thongs, fuel and beer.

On his first trip across the Savannah Way, an old shopkeeper in Borroloola had told him those were the most likely items to be stolen on the back roads of the Top End. The fuel they were carrying was chained to the backboard, and the small amount of beer was locked securely in the ute, but he would still sleep lightly.

Thongs? He didn't wear them in the bush; they were for the beach. He lay there looking out at the night, but sleep eluded him.

He rolled over and punched his pillow, and then sat up.

Claire's words earlier in the night had stayed with him. He grunted and reached for his phone. There was service out here from the tower at the small settlement at Robinson River. Guilt settled heavily in Don's chest as he opened the search engine and typed in Claire Templeton. He justified the search to himself; Claire was in his employ and had admitted to him that there was an issue in her past.

No matter what she said, he had a right to know. His first responsibility was to the paying clients on the charter. He was the owner, skipper of the boat, and responsible for everyone on board.

If there was any chance that Claire's presence on the charter would cause a problem, he needed to know.

But you could have asked her and insisted that she told you, said the little voice from his conscience, *instead of doing this surreptitious search.*

But he clicked the keys and scrolled through the hits.

Claire Templeton was a popular name, but none of the hits he opened were the Claire asleep in the swag next to his. An actor, a singer and an interior designer. He amended his search to Claire Templeton, lawyer.

Jackpot!

There was a hit on *Linked in.* Don clicked on it and scrolled through, but the woman in the photo had long dark hair. He was just about to close it but changed his mind as he looked at the photo. His eyes narrowed as he looked at familiar eyes, and the heart-shaped face.

It *was* Claire, but a dark-haired Claire without glasses. He remembered the packets of hair bleach he'd seen in her shopping bag when he'd brought her back across the river.

So big deal said his conscience. Lots of women changed their hair colour on a regular basis; that wasn't a crime.

He quickly scanned the information in the post. She'd graduated with Honours from Sydney Uni, and then gone to work at a prestigious law firm in Bligh Street, Sydney.

Hell, even he'd heard of that one. They were often mentioned on national news as handling high-profile cases.

But there were no more links from *Linked In*, and no other sites with Claire listed.

He stared outside into the dark, his mind working before he typed her name, and the name of the law firm in the search box.

Success again! A small article in a legal newsletter wishing her well in her new position as host of Impact Australia network news program. He frowned as he typed in her name and the name of the program and came up with a blank. The trail went cold.

Maybe she hadn't gone there after all.

Chapter 9

Claire lay on her back listening to every sound coming through the thin canvas of the swag. Leaves rustled, and small animals scurried around. She drew her feet up as far as she could—not that anything could get into the swag, Don had assured her—but she still stiffened at every sound, imagining a crocodile creeping into the camp. As she lay there, her eyes quickly became accustomed to the darkness as pinpricks of moonlight shone in through the seams in the swag.

After talking to Don about the charter, and the type of guests who would be on it, she was feeling sick. How could she ever have thought she could come up here and stay anonymous? Any guest from Sydney or Melbourne would recognise her immediately, blonde hair or not. All it would take would be one phone call. Or one post on social media and the media would descend in their hordes.

It didn't matter where the boat was; they'd find the *Adventurer*, and they'd find her. Her breathing hitched, and panic built in her chest. Placing her hands over her mouth, she focused on breathing in and out. There was no way she could get out of doing the charter now; she should have stayed in the relative safety and obscurity of Second Chance Bay, but Don had been kind to her; she couldn't let him down.

What the hell was she going to do? He'd sort of agreed to say she'd been up there for a while—or had he? She couldn't remember their conversation as the panicked thoughts whirled around her head.

Her breathing evened out and she closed her eyes as sleep eventually overtook her.

The studio was darker than usual, and Claire lifted her glasses and squinted so she could see the teleprompter. Strangely most of the crew had disappeared, and only the guest to be interviewed was sitting across from her. As she tried to see the words on the screen, Giselle, the production assistant, hissed at her from the front of the set. 'Stupid skank.'

Claire tried to wave her off. Giselle knew better than that; she would be on screen and blocking them from the camera. She lifted her hands, but they were too heavy to lift. She opened her mouth, but no words came out.

She looked around for the production cue sheet; she'd missed the staging meeting, she didn't know the sequence for the program. Giselle was standing there with a smile on her face and her arms folded. As she watched, Ben came and stood behind her and started kissing Giselle's neck.

'What's happening,' Claire managed to blurt out.

'You have to ask me the questions.' The guest pointed to the screen.

'No, I can't. I can't do it again.'

Giselle and Ben stood together laughing at her as the guest started to read the first question from the teleprompter. 'Were you responsible for the death of your son, Mr Hatton?'

'No!' Claire jumped to her feet and screamed. 'No, not again.'

***

Don pushed open the flap and jumped to his feet. The scream from Claire's swag had turned his blood to ice.

'Claire, I'm coming. What's wrong?' He kicked his boots out of the way and reached for the zip on her swag. Cursing because he hadn't grabbed the flashlight, he reached out in the dark trying to find where she was. His hands connected with soft curves and he pulled back quickly.

'What's wrong?' he said again. 'Is there something in here?'

118

'I'm ok…okay.' Her voice was trembling. Don reached out again but kept his hands higher this time. He touched her shoulders, and even in that light touch, he could feel her body shaking.

'What's wrong, Claire?' He kept his voice soft and calm.

'I'm sorry. I was dreaming.' Her shoulders moved beneath his fingers and the mattress rustled as she sat up. 'I'm sorry if I woke you.'

'I hope it wasn't about crocodiles?'

'No. It wasn't crocodiles.' Her voice was bitter and full of emotion.

Don sat there unsure of what to do. It wasn't really the right thing to hold her—as much as he wanted to comfort her—and she had withdrawn into her prickly shell already.

'If you're worried, we'll stop at Victoria River tomorrow night. We can get cabins there. It's pretty bas—'

'No. There's no need to change your plans just because of me. I'll be okay.' Now her voice was brisk, and she moved away to the corner of the swag. 'I'm fine. Go back to your swag.'

'No. I can tell you're upset. I'm not going to leave you. I'm still worried that it was the crocodile eyes that set you off. How about a cuppa?'

Silence.

It seemed as though she was cross with him, and for a moment Don wondered if she suspected he'd been Googling her.

No, she couldn't. But the guilt stayed with him, along with concern for the state she was in. Her vulnerability touched him deeply, and a surge of protectiveness consumed him.

'Well, I'm going to have one. I'll go and get the fire going.'

'Thank you.' The reply was so soft he hardly heard it. 'I've got some herbal tea bags in my handbag. They help me sleep.'

'Do you want me to get it out of the ute?'

'No. I've got it here. I'm wide awake now.'

Five minutes later, he had a cheery blaze going. Don filled the billy from the jerry can on the back of the ute. He didn't want to spook Claire by going down to the water's edge.

He glanced over at her, lit softly by the firelight as he hung the billy on the tripod. She had pulled her knees up to her chest in the camp chair and her arms were wrapped tightly around them. She'd passed him the teabag and then put her bag into the ute as soon as he'd unlocked it.

'Don't forget to lock it again,' she'd said.

He'd looked at her curiously. 'Will do.'

The flames snapping, and crackling provided a soothing backdrop. Don glanced at his phone. 'It's almost dawn. How would you feel about a cuppa and packing up camp, and getting an extra early start?'

'That's okay. Whatever you want to do.' Her voice held little expression and she stared at the flames.

Don couldn't help himself. While he waited for the water to boil, he crouched in front of her chair, but her eyes remained downcast.

He reached over and gently held her chin and tipped her face up. 'Claire, would it help to talk about what's bothering you?'

She held his gaze. The shadows beneath her eyes were darker than they had been yesterday, and he felt helpless, a feeling he wasn't familiar with.

'Look, I've been a sounding board for my sister over the years. I've got broad shoulders. If you want to talk, I can listen. And I won't share anything you tell me.' He tried to inject some lightness to dispel the heavy tension in the air. 'Some of the things Jenni told me over the years would make your hair curl.'

'You're a good brother. She's a very lucky girl.' Claire gave a quiet chuckle and cleared her throat, putting her hand up to her mouth, her fingers brushing his and he moved his hand away. 'I'll be okay. There's nothing I can do, apart from what I'm doing now. Circumstances won't change, but time'll go by and I'll get over it.'

'Get over it?'

She looked at him long and hard and for a moment Don thought he'd connected.

'Over what happened, and I'll get back to the real world.'

'As a lawyer?'

She shrugged. 'Who knows. I might like working on the boat. You might be stuck with me.' This time the laugh that came from her lips was forced, and Don knew she was putting on a front. 'They say a change is as good as a holiday. Don't they?'

'You probably will fall in love with the life.' He lightened the conversation. 'There's nothing like being out under the stars away out in the wilderness and seeing the Milky Way in full splendour. The Kimberley will get a hold of you. That's another reason I'm thinking about moving across there.'

'You really think you will?'

'Yeah. At the end of this trip, I'll probably take the boat back to the Gulf and work on her over there. Spend some time with Mum when she gets home, have Christmas with the family, and then head back over to the Kimberleys.'

'What about the ute?

'It can stay at Wyndham. I'll need a work vehicle when I move over there.'

'So we won't be doing this drive back?'

'Probably not. I've got to put some more thought into it yet, but don't worry, we'll get you back to the Bay. Besides you might be over the Savannah Way by the time we get to the coast anyway.'

'So you won't have any charters over the summer?'

The billy boiled over and the fire hissed as the water hit the coals. 'No, we can't charter in the wet. Too unpredictable.'

'How do you mean?'

Don glanced up at her as he poured the water onto their teabags. 'Swollen rivers, gushing waterfalls and tropical thunderstorms most afternoons. It's not safe.'

'It would be the best time to see it, maybe.'

'It is. And that's when the air tours get most of the business.'

'It sounds majestic.' Claire's voice was brighter now.

'That's a word that's often used to describe the tours. We've had some fabulous reviews on Trip Adviser for our charter.'

'Our? You have a business partner?'

'No. just a figure of speech. It's just me.' Don laughed and shook his head as he passed her the cup. She lowered her legs, and he smiled as she examined the ground before she put her bare feet down. 'You're really not used to the outdoors, are you?'

Her smile was bright, and he was pleased to see the sadness that had surrounded her seemed to have lifted. 'No, but I plan to change that.' She gestured around. The sun wasn't far off rising, and the sky was getting lighter in the east. 'In fact, I already am!' She regarded him as she sat down and picked up his mug.

'You plan to travel around for a while?'

Again, that shrug. 'A few months.'

A comfortable silence descended for a few minutes as they drank their tea.

At least Claire looked a bit happier now. For a while, she'd looked like she was on the verge of tears. As the sky lightened the shadows lifted and her colour seemed to come back. She was a beautiful woman; green cat's eyes slightly tipped at the corners in a heart-shaped face with lips that were lush and full.

Kissable popped into his head.

As her cup moved to those lips discomfort filled Don when he realised Claire was looking back at him. He dropped his gaze to his mug, but she reached over and put her hand on his arm. 'Thank you for being kind. I know I can be moody, but I do appreciate it.'

'Nothing more than any decent person would do,' he huffed. Don stood and tipped out the dregs of his tea before getting the thermos from the back of the ute. No point wasting the boiling water; it would do them as they travelled today.

Claire stood and stretched as he tipped the billy and poured the boiling water in. He dragged his eyes away from the strip of bare skin that appeared between her T-shirt and the waistband of her cargo pants.

The reaction he had wasn't one that a gentleman should have in the middle of nowhere with an attractive woman. He turned his back and stayed over at the ute pretending to check the ropes. By the time he turned back around, Claire had disappeared back into the swag.

***

As she sat in the swag and gathered her toiletries bag—not that she'd needed that so far—Claire thought about the stupid dream. It was the fright of seeing the crocodile that had given her the nightmare; the fright had stimulated her brain and set other thoughts swirling. Something about the dream tugged at her, but she couldn't remember what it was. All she could see was that poor man sitting in the interview chair. She pushed open the swag and carried the small bag over to the ute.

It didn't take long to pack up camp. Claire was learning new skills each hour that passed. Watching Don hang the billy over the fire and seeing how he held it to tip the water. Learning how to roll up her swag had been fun, but she'd been conscious of his proximity as he'd leaned over to show her how to pull the tags tight. He smelled good; fresh and clean like washing that had come in from the sunshine. He'd put on a clean T-shirt, and Claire considered going down to the river and having a wash to freshen up.

She stood beside the ute as Don loaded the table and chairs. There was no point in being a coward; she was going to have to toughen up before she got on his boat.

With a determined and deep breath, she grabbed her soap and a face washer and headed for the small stand of trees. It was a far cry from any bathroom she'd used before, but she coped.

She came out of the small copse of trees and headed down the hill towards the water, keeping a wary eye on the grass and the loose reddish sand at the edge of the river. As she paused a few metres back from the edge, a huge splash came from the other side. She jumped and put her hand to her chest, but the splash was immediately followed by the roar of an engine. She watched fascinated as a large four-wheel drive vehicle ploughed across the river, about fifty metres downstream at the crossing, with a huge arc of spray on either side. Waiting until it had disappeared up the hill, Claire looked around at the river before gingerly stepping to the edge. She bent down, her eyes fixed on the water in front of her. She widened her eyes; it was so clear, she could see the flat brown stones on the bottom as the water trickled over them. It was only about twenty centimetres deep, nowhere for a crocodile to hide.

Feeling very brave she leaned forward with her hands cupped and washed her face.

'You're getting brave.' Don's voice from behind brought a smile to her lips.

'I am. But you did come to guard me.' Claire gestured to the river. 'I didn't realise how pretty it was out here.' She shook her hands dry as she looked across to the other side. The sand there was not red, and closer to the colour of sand that she was used to. A lush patch of bright green grass ran down one side of the small cove and into the water. The sun was getting higher and sunlight sparkled on the water that was flowing faster on the other side of the river. Small stands of shrubs with a pale pink flower edged the grass, and lacy cobwebs held tiny droplets of water like diamonds.

Don came down and stood beside her before crouching and washing his face and hands. His eyes glinted with mirth as she reached down and rinsed her face again.

'Are you missing a bathroom? There's a secluded copse over there.'

'I know.' She stood up straight and grinned at him. 'I already found it.'

'You're doing well.' He turned and held out his hand. 'Come on, we'll get going. About six hours more and the worst part of the trip is over.'

His fingers were strong and warm, and Claire didn't let go of them as they walked up the hill. A warm feeling curled in her chest, and she squeezed his fingers when they reached the ute.

'Thank you,' she whispered. Unable to help herself she reached and brushed her lips across his cheek

'What for?' Surprise crossed his face as she stepped back but Don kept hold of her hand as she looked up at him.

'For being a good man.'

His laugh was self-conscious as he let go of her hand and flicked her cheek with a gentle finger.

'Thank *you* for keeping me company.'

##

By the time they'd done the third river crossing, Claire was enjoying herself. Looking up the middle of a wide river as the ute ploughed through metre-deep water was exhilarating. It was almost like being on a boat. As they went up the hill on the other side she frowned. 'How come the motor doesn't conk out?'

Don grinned back at her and pointed to the funny black thing on the side of the windscreen. 'That's what the snorkel's for. It stops the engine ingesting the water.'

Claire shook her head. 'This has been an education so far. Does anyone ever float away?'

He nodded, and she widened her eyes.

'Often. Wait until you see the abandoned car wrecks along the side of the road from now to Borroloola. The retrieval of breakdowns keeps the local mechanic in business. Cars, camper trailers and utes—the road gets worse from here. The grader from Borroloola doesn't get this far out.'

'It's a whole new world out here.' She folded her arms. 'And I'm loving it more every minute.'

And it wasn't just because they were isolated and not seeing other people, taking away her fear of being recognised. She was enjoying being with Don and was gaining more respect for him each time he safely manoeuvred the car through deep ditches, washouts and bull dust, and through rivers.

I'm even getting the lingo right, she thought with a grin.

The fragments of that stupid dream in the early hours had finally left her and she felt foolish for waking him up. When he'd come into the swag and his fingers had brushed against her breast in the dark, a jolt of awareness had hit her. All she'd wanted was for his arms to go around her and comfort her. She'd been hyperaware of him ever since and hadn't been able to resist kissing his cheek. It had been tempting to brush her lips over his mouth, but she'd thought better of it. It was simply a thank you kiss for a man who was showing her kindness and friendship. And a man who'd given her a job.

She had to remember that. Once they were on the boat, Don would be her boss.

Then these stupid feelings that were building in her would have to be put aside. Don McDougal came from a different world to hers—not that she was sure what her world was at the moment.

One consolation—as strange as it seemed—trying to put him out of her mind had taken the worry of what had happened in Sydney into the back of her mind.

She reached for the small pillow that Don had put on the seat and leaned her head against it as the landscape went by.

Chapter 10

They reached the small township of Borroloola late morning. As Don had said, they'd passed abandoned cars and trailers covered in red dust. They'd stopped once for a cup of tea and a snack, and she'd helped him hold the jerry can up and fill the fuel tank with diesel.

As they drove into the small town, Don turned to her. 'Do you want to stop? Do you need anything?'

Claire went to shake her head, and then she thought of Aunt Bea and how she'd be worrying about her. 'If you want to have a break, I wouldn't mind finding a public phone and calling my aunt if we've got time to stop.'

Don flicked her a glance. 'No need to worry about a public phone. You can use my mobile. I was going to call in at the mechanic and get him to put the ute up on the hoist, just to check the suspension. I can't see anything wrong, but that was a pretty loud bang when we went into that bull dust yesterday.'

'Thank you. There's service here?'

'Yeah.' He turned the ute off the main—now tarred—road and drove a hundred metres past some old houses until they reached a small row of shops. Claire was surprised to see many of the businesses were closed and the front windows boarded up. She pointed to a grocery store that had a high wire fence around it, with a gate at the front that was propped open. A group of children, surrounded by half a dozen mangey dogs, were playing on the red dirt.

'Why are the windows boarded up?' she asked curiously.

'There's a few social issues out here.'

She turned and watched as they passed more buildings with fences and boarded-up windows and it reminded her of a program they'd done on similar issues earlier in the year. She'd been nominated for the Walkley for that program.

Don turned into the workshop yard and parked the ute. Cars in various states of disrepair lined the cyclone fence, but the building was freshly painted, and the workshop area looked tidy from where Claire was sitting. A red kelpie came running out, barking madly. 'Don't worry about the dog. She's harmless.' He turned off the engine and leaned forward and pulled his phone out of his back pocket. 'Hopefully, Jim can look at the wheel straight up. Hop out and stretch your legs, it'll be a few hours until we hit the Stuart Highway.' He grinned, and the tanned skin around blue eyes crinkled. 'Sick of being on the road yet?'

Claire opened the door and Don came around to her side. 'No. I'm not. It's a whole new experience.' This time she grinned up at him as she stood close to her. 'A walk will be good. Those ute seats get a bit hard after a while.'

'They do.' He handed her his phone and pointed to a takeaway shop a couple of doors further along. 'Coffee's not bad there if you want to get a couple after you make your call.'

'Thanks. How do you have yours?'

'Cappuccino with two sugars. Thanks.'

Claire reached in for her bag and hugged it tight to her chest with one hand, Don's phone in the other. As she walked away, he called out to her. 'Three two, three two, three two, to get into the phone.'

She waved in acknowledgement and headed for the store, deciding to order the coffee first. Pushing open the door, she stepped into the dark and cool interior, the smell of fried food overpowering. Despite the oily smell, she was surprised to see a display of fresh-made sandwiches and homemade cakes in a small refrigerated cabinet next to the counter.

'What would you like, love?' A woman with a purple apron covering her dress, and an immaculate hairstyle smiled across the counter.

Claire looked at the sandwiches. If she bought some lunch, it would save a stop in an hour or so, to prepare something. So far, apart from a few homemade biscuits, she'd contributed little to the road trip.

She certainly hadn't been a fount of scintillating conversation or happy company, and she'd cut Don's sleep short with that stupid dream. The least she could do was buy him lunch.

'Two salad rolls please, and two cappuccinos. To take away.'

'You in a rush love?' A waft of strong perfume came from the woman as she moved to the cash register.

'Not really. I've got at least twenty minutes.'

'I'll make you a couple of fresh ones. Those premade ones will be snapped up by the boys from the mine when they come in for lunch.'

'The mine?'

The woman laughed. 'You must have come in from the east.'

Claire nodded.

'Well, if you're heading west now, you'll get a shock, four-lane highway past the mine for quite a few miles. It's the boys from there that keep my shop going. And the grey nomies and the fishermen going out to King Ash Bay.' She picked up a couple of bread rolls and walked over to the bench. 'What about you, love? Where are you heading?'

'We're going—' Claire's breath caught as she looked down at her face staring up at her from the cover of a glossy gossip magazine.

SYBIL HARRIS FLEES TO THE COTE D'AZUR, the lead headline read.

'Um…to Wyndham.'

The woman chatted on about the coast, and the road, but Claire's ears were buzzing.

'I'll be back in a minute.' She pushed open the door and pulled out the plastic chair at the table outside the shop. As she tried to settle, she looked over to the workshop. The ute was now up on the hoist and Don was talking to the mechanic.

The media were still on her case. She huffed a bitter laugh. At least they had her out of the country. Surprisingly, that thought calmed her.

She took a deep breath and took Don's phone from her pocket. Talking to Aunty Bea would help too.

She typed in the password and her eyes widened as the screen opened to Linked In. And a photo of her, taken when she worked at Baker and Baker in Bligh Street.

What the hell?

***

The strut to the shockie had a slight bend in it, but Jim assured him that it would last the trip.

'No prob, mate. If you're in a hurry just replace it when you get there. I haven't got one in stock, and it'll take a week or so to get one up from Melbourne. Even longer probably.' He pointed to a Rodeo ute with a smashed back window. 'That poor bugger's been waiting three weeks for his new glass. He was loaded up with fresh meat and fruit to take out to Roper River, and his fridge was full. The missus and I ate salad for a week!'

Don paid the bill and then backed the ute out. Claire was walking back towards him carrying one coffee and a brown paper bag. He jumped out and opened the door for her as she crossed to the ute.

She shoved the coffee into his hand and threw the brown paper bag onto the seat before getting into the ute and staring stonily ahead. She put her bag onto the floor and after he'd closed her door, and climbed into the driver's seat, she handed his phone back to him.

'Did you get onto your aunt?' he asked carefully as he started the car. As he looked over his shoulder to reverse out, he glanced at Claire. Her lips were set, and there were two spots of colour high on her cheeks. 'Everything was okay?'

'She's fine.' The tone was clipped. She gestured to the seat. 'If you're hungry I got you a salad roll.'

'Good plan, thanks. There's a nice grassy area at Cape Crawford. We'll stop there. It's about an hour away.'

As they drove along the highway, kindly sealed by the McArthur River mine, there wasn't a word spoken.

As the hour of silence passed, Don's temper built.

Talk about moody.

Even at her crankiest, Jenni would always say what was bothering her, usually accompanied by a good thump. Claire was obviously upset about something, but opposite to Jenni, it looked like she bottled things up.

He stared ahead at the road. You could cut the air in the ute with a knife. It was at least another ten hours to where he'd planned to stay tonight, and then a relatively short trip across to Wyndham in the morning. He couldn't let it go; if Claire was going to be moody like this on the boat—for no good reason that he could see—he was going to have to speak to her. He wouldn't let her moods impact on the guests.

And he wasn't looking forward to that.

But yet beneath his temper, there was a part of him that worried about her. It was because he found her so bloody attractive; he had to remind himself that the sad vulnerability might be calculated. Anyone who could switch moods like that had a problem.

He had to keep that in his head and get over the physical reaction to Claire.

But maybe she was frightened of something?

Just after eleven, Don pulled the ute up on the road outside the hotel at Cape Crawford. The grassy area was one of the nicest places to stop on the journey west, and the amenities were clean and open to travellers. Claire had the door open, her bag tucked beneath her arm, and was striding across to the building before he had turned the engine off.

With a shrug, he picked up the lunch bag and took it over to one of the tables sheltered by the huge trees. He put the empty coffee cup in the bin, sat down and waited for her to come out before he opened the bag. The silence was broken as a helicopter took off from the paddock beside the hotel. The hotel, the shack where the helicopter flights were booked for sightseeing over the Lost City, and half a dozen houses, were the only buildings in the tiny settlement at the junction of the Carpentaria and Tablelands Highways.

A good ten minutes later, she walked across the grass and passed another coffee to him. Her hair was wet, and she'd changed her T-shirt. She must have made use of the public showers.

'Thank you.' He gestured to the bag. 'I waited for you.'

'I'm not hungry.' She sat and folded her arms, looking around at the picnic area.

'It's a good place to stop.'

When she didn't reply, Don reached for the bag and took out one of the salad rolls.

'If you're not going to eat, I'll put yours in the camp fridge.'

'Whatever.'

Don's family knew that it took a lot to fire his temper, but he knew they all would have recognised the set of his jaw and his slow movements as he put the bread roll back down on the paper.

'May I have a word?'

She lifted her chin and stared at him.

He stared back. 'I'm going, to be frank here, Claire. Your moodiness is pissing me off. One minute you're telling me how "kind" I am and kissing me, the next minute, you're playing no speakies and sending me dagger glares every time I open my mouth.'

'I did not.'

'What? Kiss me or the filthy looks?'

'Not a real kiss.' Her chin was as high as his.

A real kiss was something he might try one day. Maybe that would stir up the calm and controlled Claire Templeton. He wondered what it would be like to peel away layer by layer and find the true woman beneath that exterior.

'As your employer, I have to say something. I can't risk you being like this on the *Adventurer*.'

'Like what?'

'Oh for Pete's sake, Claire, Like this! Snarky when you do deign to talk to me.'

'I can give you my word you I won't be snarky with the guests on the boat.' She moved across the seat closer to him and lowered her chin, so they were almost nose to nose.

'Unless…'

Despite his temper, he couldn't help but notice the coconut fragrance coming from her damp hair. 'Unless what?' He held her gaze and didn't budge. It was hard not to let his eyes drop to her lips that were millimetres away from his.

'Unless they stalk me on social media.'

He frowned. 'What the hell are you talking about.'

And then the guilt punched in as he remembered she'd used his phone at Borroloola. That's when her mood changed. When she'd come back from the shop and making her call.

'Fair enough.'

'Fair enough? That's all you've got to say.' Her face came closer and he could smell peppermint toothpaste on her breath.

She turned her head to look past him and moved back a little.

He put one hand on her arm and cupped her cheek with the other. 'Tell me what's wrong, Claire?'

Her eyes met his again and a sucker punch hit his gut as tears glittered on her long lashes.

'I'm sorry. I wanted to know more about you. You fascinate me, and I wondered if I knew any more about you, I could help.'

'You could have asked.' Her voice trembled.

'I did. A couple of times.'

Her soft sigh blew on his lips, and without thinking, Don dipped his head and laid his lips lightly on hers. She didn't move away. His fingers tightened a little bit on her face and he lifted his other hand and cupped her cheeks with both hands. This time the kiss was deeper... and longer. Relief flooded through him when her lips parted beneath his and her hands crept around his neck.

Don's pulse hammered as her tongue brushed his briefly. Claire drew back and lowered her hand to his chest. He put his hand over it.

'I'm sorry for being so hard to get on with but seeing myself on *Linked In* on your phone brought me undone. And the magazine in the shop, and then Aunt Bea told me that reporters had been to the aged care home wanting to talk to her.' She lifted her head and her face was awash with tears.

Don reached out and used his thumb to stop another tear from falling.

Her voice hitched in a sob. 'And then to know that you knew all about me and hadn't said anything.'

'Whoa, Claire. I don't know *all* about you. Any more than what you told me. You were a lawyer. I don't know why you're up here, and I don't know why reporters would be trying to find you. Or what magazine you're talking about. I do know you're running from something, and in my defence rather than curiosity, it was more worry that drove me to look you up.'

She pulled back from him, and for a moment he thought she was still mad at him, but she dug in her bag and pulled out a magazine.

'I saw it in the shop at Borroloola. It was the last one, so I bought it.' Her laugh held no humour. 'Not that anyone way up there would have recognised me off the cover.'

He held his hand out as she passed him the magazine and he looked down at a photo of a dark-haired Claire on the cover.

Chapter 11

'The *Cote d'Azur*?' Don lifted his head after he'd looked at her picture on the front of the trashy magazine. 'Second Chance Bay is a long way from the Mediterranean.'

Claire nodded. Don still had hold of her hand. He'd put the magazine on the table and so far, had only looked at the headline and hadn't opened it to read the article.

'And who's this Sybil Harris with your photo on a beach in France?'

'It's a photo of me, and it was taken at Ettalong on the Central Coast last summer. They've photoshopped me onto a French beach! The media will do anything to beef up a good story. Trust me, I've been there and, sad to say, part of a team that's done things that were just as unfair.' She took her hand from his and tucked her hair behind her ear. 'Sybil Harris is my work name. I thought it was better to change it for the show, after being at the law firm.'

'You did leave the law firm and go to a television network.' He looked at her sheepishly. 'I'll be honest I did Google that.'

'It's okay. I know you were only trying to help. It's only been a few weeks since it happened, and I think I'm gradually coming to terms with it. My real name is Claire Sybil Harris-Templeton. Thank goodness none of them have discovered that yet.'

'Is there a chance they'll pick that up?'

'Probably. Maybe I was stupid to run away but I was so upset about that poor man, and all of the garbage that the media was making up, I couldn't cope with being in the city.'

'Changed your hair colour?'

She looked down and nodded. 'And cut my hair with manicure scissors in a hotel room. I was kidding myself. I still look the same, don't I?'

Don leaned back and looked at the magazine and then at Claire. 'There's a resemblance, but she—you—could pass for your sister. Or even just someone who looks like you.'

'That's a relief.' Her shoulders relaxed, and she smiled as he took her hand again. Holding Don's hand grounded her. She refused to think about the kiss they'd shared. 'I was worried back at the house when Matt said I reminded him of someone. You didn't seem to see it.'

'I've never seen'—he let go of her hand and flicked open the magazine— 'Impact Australia.'

'I was the host for six months.'

'I'm out to sea on charters most of the time, and to be honest, I hate the way television has gone lately. Stupid reality shows, and the news reporting that's not even news.'

'I know. There are no standards. It's all about chasing the dollar these days. I'm sorry to say I was a part of it. I was very trusting and naïve. And I guess it was ego that kicked in when I was offered the job.'

'Tell me what happened.' His thigh was warm against hers as he looked at the article. and Claire closed her eyes for a moment, savouring the pressure against her leg.

'It's a long story, and we should get back on the road. You said we've still got a lot of hours on the road today.'

'You're right.' He handed her the magazine and glanced at his watch. 'We will, but on one condition. You eat your lunch now, and then you can tell me as we drive.' He reached out and held her shoulders gently. 'But only if you're happy to tell me. I don't want to have forced you into it by that *Linked In* stuff.'

Claire dropped her head to Don's shoulder and it was like going home. His hand came up and cupped the back of her head and she breathed in the same fresh smell as she had early this morning. She closed his eyes again as his fingers gently smoothed her hair.

'I'm happy to. It will be good to share. I haven't told anyone else. Aunt Bea knows a little bit about what happened, but she thinks I've gone on a holiday to take some time out.'

'Okay. Come on then. Eat up. I'll just go to the amenities, and then grab us another coffee before we go. You okay here by yourself for five?'

She nodded, feeling better than she had for a month. 'Of course, I am. I don't think there's a media horde hiding here. And Don? Thank you.'

'You've got to stop all this thanking me all the time, you know.' He grinned, and her heart gave a little kick. 'Wait until I get you on the boat, you'll see me in my true tyrannical form. Now eat your lunch and I'll take you on another scenic tour of the Top End.'

Claire did as she was told and finished the salad roll. As she ate she flicked through the article in the magazine. The story was so bad, and so way off base, she even smiled at times.

The mystery that everyone seemed to be reporting on now, was where had Sybil Harris gone? France? Morocco? New York?

I wish.

They didn't seem to be focusing on the show any more, that was old news.

Hopefully.

She shook her head as she took the scraps across to the bin.

Talk about gutter journalism, photoshopping an old photo of her and saying she was in France!

By the time Don came back, and handed her a coffee, Claire was feeling a lot better.

'It happened on the program one night.' Claire looked across at Don and he reached over and squeezed her hand in brief encouragement. She looked down at her fingers when he let them go. How could a simple brush of skin against skin send a jolt though her whole body?

They were back on the road. A much better road, single lane, but at least it was tarred. She stared ahead, reliving the events of that night. 'I'd missed the staging meeting. They changed the time of the meeting and the production assistant stuffed up and left me out of the email saying it had been brought forward a couple of hours. I'd missed a couple before and it had been okay. As long as I had the running sheet and my research was up to date, I knew I'd be fine.' Claire pulled her knees up and hugged them.

'Could the lack of an email have been deliberate, do you think?'

Claire shook her head. 'No, Giselle is a top-notch assistant. She just about grovelled after the meeting when she realised it was her fault that I missed it.'

'Fair enough.'

'I should have been fine with what I had. It might sound like ego kicking in, but I was a damn good reporter. I was even nominated for a Walkley this year.'

Don whistled. 'Even *I* know what that is.'

'I went to introduce the guest and when I read the teleprompter—that's the screen that flashes up the script between me and the camera—it threw me. As soon as I saw his name I panicked. Inside anyway.' She bit her lip as she recalled Ross Timmins sitting across from her. 'He wasn't the guest that I'd been expecting. I managed to stay calm on the outside. He had such a kind face, and his eyes were sad.'

Claire had been expecting to ask some hard questions of a CEO of a charity where money had gone missing. The federal corruption agency had been investigating him, but the CEO had so far managed to evade any charges; she'd been surprised when he'd agreed to be interviewed. Unbeknown to him, the network had been given some crucial information, and that night's show was the night she was going to present that information to him.

And expose him.

On air.

In front of the nation.

Her stomach churned, and she felt ill. Instead Ross Timmins had been sitting there.

'I had no idea who he was,' Claire continued as she brought Don up to speed. 'But I trusted my production crew and the research team, so I asked him the questions as they came up on the teleprompter. Questions about his young son, and how he'd died. Questions that intimated that he hadn't done as much as he could have seeking medical treatment. It was loosely linked to the charity that was being investigated. I'll never, ever, forget the look on his face.'

'So, what happened?' Don asked quietly.

'That's the problem. I don't know.' Claire dropped her gaze to her hands. She hadn't even been aware that they were clutched tightly in her lap. Her knuckles were white, and she eased her fingers apart and flexed them.

'We went to an ad break, and he collapsed in tears. Giselle and Ben ran over to him, and they had to help him off the set.' She closed her eyes as she remembered his stricken face. 'I was left sitting there stunned. I brought him to that state and on national television.'

'You didn't cause it. Your team did. Or whoever wrote the questions.'

'I should have been at the meeting. The crazy thing was that when they pulled up the teleprompter none of the questions that I'd asked were there. My running sheet disappeared, and I had no proof that I'd been given the wrong questions.'

'You were set up.'

'I was. But even I started to doubt my recollection of what had happened when it hit the fan. I had no evidence of anything. I simply looked like a hard bitch. When I finally stood up the network CEO was next to the camera with a face like thunder. Ben was there, holding his arm, holding him back. The boss looked like he was ready to attack me.'

'Then?'

'I got hauled into his office. I explained about the teleprompter and the running sheet, but he didn't believe me. It looked like I had gone out for glory off my own bat. Anyone who knows me, knows I wouldn't have done that. Even Ben didn't support me.'

'Ben?'

'The director. We were sort of seeing each other.' Claire bit her lip and stared ahead at a large cloud of dust. 'What's that?'

'Cattle muster. They do it by helicopter out here.'

Having her attention taken away from the memory of that night helped her breathing return to normal.

'Did you lose your job? Is that why you're up here?'

'No. Would you believe the ratings went through the roof, and all of a sudden I was a golden-haired girl.'

'I don't understand?' Don frowned as he slowed the car as a couple of horseman waved at them.

'With the program, and the station. The CEO ended up being delighted. I was even offered a bonus. It was the media that turned on me. I was made out to be the hard-nosed bitch who would do anything for ratings. Sybil Harris, arch bitch.' She shook her head as Don backed the speed off more as a mob of cattle appeared a hundred metres ahead. 'The headlines, the social media, the phone calls. You've got no idea what it was like. It was as though I was a criminal. They camped outside my house. I had to leave. I was mortified.'

'Have you quit?'

153

'No, I took a leave of absence. No pay. But my contract is up for renewal in a month.'

'Will the network renew?'

'Probably.' She shrugged. 'I don't know, but whatever they decide, I've come to a decision. I won't go back. It's not what I'd expected. It's not what I wanted it to be.' She turned to face him as Don turned the engine off. 'I don't know what I'll do yet. Job wise, that is.'

Hundreds of beasts milled in the paddock on either side of the road. The thudding of helicopter blades filled the air. Two horsemen were rounding up the stragglers that had broken out onto the bitumen road.

'I took that job because I thought as part of the team, I could make a difference. We did make a difference on a number of our reports, but this one's disillusioned me. I can't go back.'

'Not even to vindicate yourself, and find out who set you up? Have you got any ideas?' Don reached over and put his arm around her, and she rested her head on his shoulder.

A fragment of memory flitted through Claire's thoughts, but she couldn't hold onto it.

'No.'

'It has to be someone on the crew. It shouldn't be too hard to work out.'

'Perhaps not, but I've taken the coward's way out. I'm not going back to Sydney until it all dies down.'

Chapter 12

As they turned onto the Stuart Highway and headed south for a short while before turning west again, Claire didn't stir. She'd been asleep for a while, obviously exhausted by going over what had happened.

Bastards, Don thought. It wasn't hard to see that Claire was a good person, and that her motivation for taking the job had probably been idealistic. She'd been shafted, and the media had come in after her blood. As she'd said, anything to improve ratings; it was such an artificial world. Give him the freedom of the sea and the outback any day.

He glanced over at Claire again. Her lips were gently parted, her eyes closed, and her chest rose and fell with each breath she took. Her fingers held the pillow that she'd propped up against the window. When she'd yawned and dug out the pillow, Don had changed his mind about the route they'd take. It meant a rough road for a while but would cut a good three hundred and fifty kilometres off the trip.

Claire woke up as soon as they hit the dirt. She rubbed her eyes and looked around. 'Roadworks?'

'No. I've decided to take a shortcut. I'll head for Top Springs tonight, and it means we'll get to the boat a bit earlier tomorrow.

'You're the boss.' She rubbed her eyes again and stretched. 'How long was I asleep?'

'A couple of hours. How do you feel?'

'Much better. Thanks for being a sounding board.'

'My pleasure. Sorry, the ute's going to shudder for a while.' Don slowed down as they hit more corrugations. 'Listen, I've been thinking about what you said the other day about being on the boat.'

'What do you mean?' Claire tipped her head to the side and her hair fell over her shoulder. His fingers itched to hold her close again, and he looked away.

She was an employee for God's sake. He shouldn't have kissed her back at Cape Crawford.

And now he had a dilemma. He'd shown her sympathy, he knew her story and he'd given into the attraction he'd felt, breaking his cardinal rule of not getting involved with employees.

What he'd been thinking about broke that rule and every other one he'd ever made about dealing with staff.

He grinned ruefully. 'The favour you asked, about me saying you'd been on the boat for months.'

'Yes?' she said slowly.

'The guests on the boat are usually wealthy, savvy businessmen and from what you've said about the high-profile show, and the media circus afterwards, I think there's a pretty good chance someone onboard will see the resemblance.'

Her face fell. 'So, you're saying you don't want me on the charter?'

'No, I'm going to suggest something that should dispel any idea that you're Sybil—?'

'Harris,' she filled in for him.

'Yes, Sybil Harris.' He shot her a sideways glance. Her eyes were already on him.

'Tell me?'

'I will when we pull up for the night. Not long now.'

***

By the time they pulled up just before dark, Claire was feeling much better. Sharing with Don what had happened had been cathartic, and being able to be honest about the mutual attraction had taken away the emotional undercurrent from their conversation. This time they worked well together. Claire knew what had to come off the back of the ute and managed to set up her swag.

'I'll do that for you,' Don said, but she knocked back his offer to help.

'No. I'd like to see if I can do it. There's a new me after today. I'm going to have a go at new things and take some risks.'

They'd had to stop for cattle a couple of times on the last leg of the trip. The last hundred kilometres had been flat and straight, and the road wasn't too bad. Red dust and dry yellow grass on each side, along with low scrubby trees. As they came into Top Springs Don turned to her.

'There's a camping area at the back of the pub, plus some cabins. So, cabin or swag? Your choice.'

'Swag. There was no point bringing them on the ute if you were going to take a cabin. And I was comfortable last night.'

'Good stuff,' he said with a grin.' And the best part is, the pub does an amazing meal, and there's a camp kitchen too so we won't have to light a fire.'

'What about crocodiles?' she asked, but her tone was joking.

159

Don spread his arms wide and spun around. 'Do you see a river?'

'Just checking.'

He reached over and helped her up as she stood up from pegging down her swag. 'Nightmares tonight?'

'I hope not.'

Once they were set up, Don pointed out the amenities block at the back of the hotel. 'Do you want to have a shower before dinner?'

'Do I have time?"

'Sure. I'll go in and book a table, and then I'll come back and wash some of the road dirt off too. Might as well make use of them.' He chuckled. 'Get value for our twenty dollars.'

Claire went to the ute and picked up her toiletries bag and towel. She opened her suitcase and pulled out clean underwear and one of the dresses she'd packed. Holding her handbag in one hand, and clutching her towel, clothes and toiletries in the other, she walked across to the small amenities block.

It was basic, but clean and the water was hot. She stood beneath the shower and tipped her head back, rinsing the shampoo from her hair. Telling Don what had led to her arrival in Second Chance Bay had been cathartic, and she wondered what he was going to suggest. It was a worry that he thought she might be recognised, but she could simply shake her head and deny being Sybil Harris as she went about her new job on the boat.

A little frisson of nerves tugged at her as she turned the taps off and reached for the towel. Was she being naïve again?

##

Admiration filled Don's eyes as Claire walked back to the campsite. She put her head down as the warm evening breeze blew tendrils of damp hair onto her face. She put her dusty clothes in the ute and tucked her handbag beneath her arm before she turned to him.

'I didn't realise how much dust had settled on me. The water was red!'

'You'll get used to it. It's one of the things that our guests comment on most when we go for the treks.' Don held the door of the hotel open for her, and Claire smiled as the cool air hit her face.

Surprisingly the room was crowded and there was a small queue over at the counter. Instinctively she dropped her head, and let her hair fall across her face.

What am I going to be like back in the city? she wondered. *Will my life ever be normal again?*

If anyone had told her a month ago that she'd be sitting in a pub on a dirt road in the middle of the Northern Territory, and sleeping in a swag, she would have waved a dismissive, manicured hand.

Claire looked down at her fingers as they sat at the table. Her nails were clipped short and square now, and unpainted. She hadn't worn make-up since she'd left Sydney.

But the change was good. It was as though she was morphing back into the real Claire Templeton again. A place where she was comfortable in her own skin.

'What would you like to drink?' Don nodded over to the bistro. 'We'll let the crowd clear before we order our meal.'

'Just a soft drink, thanks. Lime and soda will be fine.' She wasn't going to risk anything that might set off another nightmare tonight.

As Don walked over to the bar, her gaze stayed on him. A shame he'd added a button-through shirt to the clean black jeans he'd changed into. The muscles that his usual T-shirts clung to lovingly weren't as obvious tonight. But his height and broad shoulders, and the way he held himself were just as appealing. Don was a strong man, both physically and character-wise, and Claire had appreciated the concern he had shown to her. She also appreciated what a fine-looking man he was. As he stood at the bar chatting to the barman, she wondered what his solution was going to be. When she'd thought that he was going to suggest that she didn't come on the charter, her first reaction had been disappointment.

Drumming her fingers on the wooden table top, she waited for him to come back with their drinks. By the time he walked back and placed her soft drink and a glass of beer on the table, her nerves were zinging.

'Thank you.' Claire picked up her drink and took a long sip as Don sat down. As soon as he'd had a drink, she sat up straight and put her hands on the table.

'So tell me this idea of yours. How do we get rid of any idea that I'm Sybil Harris.'

'Okay.'

She waited.

He put his beer on the table and leaned back in his chair. Fresh soap and a hint of aftershave wafted across to her and she looked up. Don had shaved, and his tanned skin looked smooth. It was just as attractive as the dark stubble that had appeared over the past couple of days. Claire curled her fingers and dropped her head, to avoid the temptation of reaching out and running her fingers along his chin to see if it felt as good as it looked.

Oh, for goodness sake!

'Okay ...' His deep voice interrupted her thoughts as she chastised herself.

Claire lifted her head to meet this gaze. 'You've got me worried, Don. If you've changed your mind about me coming, I can get back to Second Chance Bay. I should have told you my story before we left.'

'No. It's fine. This is what I am proposing.' He chuckled, and Claire frowned.

'What's so funny?'

'I'm not actually proposing. That was a poor choice of a word.'

'What?' She stared at him, totally confused now.

'The whole crew on this charter is new. New chef, new deckhands'—he smiled— 'and a new hostess.'

'So your idea is…?'

'How would you feel about being Claire McDougal?'

'What?' If a jaw could drop, Claire's did.

Don put his hand up. 'Not in reality. Just for the trip. And it will explain why I'm teaching you the job from scratch. Most of the crew would expect that I'd have an experienced hostess on board. We'll tell the crew that I couldn't get one in time— they would have seen the recent ads at the agency in Darwin when they signed on—and that my wife of six months agreed to do it. Not only to help me out, but because she was missing me so much. Does that sound feasible?'

Claire sat back and crossed her arms as she looked at him, not sure what to think. 'So …' she said slowly. 'Would the skipper and his wife share a cabin?'

'If we wanted to be convincing, we would. But there's a small single bed in my cabin. And you will have the hostess cabin for your privacy too. The deckhand's and chef's cabins are at the back of the boat. The hostess is up by the wheelhouse, where my cabin is. Besides, most nights I'll be up on watch, so you won't have to put up with my snoring.'

***

By the look Claire cast his way, she might have been thinking it was a ploy to get her between the sheets.

Don had standards. On his boat, and in his personal life. Okay, so he was attracted, but if she thought he'd try and pull that she didn't know him well enough yet.

Yet.

She cleared her throat as she shifted her gaze back to him. 'Okay. It sounds as though it's a good solution. I think?'

'Claire, I have a rule. Business and pleasure don't mix. Not while we're on the boat anyway.' He lowered his voice and reached for her hand. Claire watched as his thumb rubbed her open palm. 'But I'll also be up front with you. In case you hadn't noticed, I think you are a very interesting woman, and when we go back to the Bay maybe we can explore our relationship a little more.' He laughed. 'Then again, you'll have seen me in action by then, and I'll probably yell at you a hundred times.'

'So, you'd yell at your new wife, would you?' Her tone was prudish, but it was tempered by a cheeky grin.

'It's good to see you smile, Claire. Really smile.'

'I'm happy for you to do that. If you're really sure. You don't owe me anything, you know.'

'I want to. It's a horrible situation for you to be in.

'I know. And I've handled it really badly so far.' She sighed. 'But I can see light at the end of the tunnel. I'll go back to Sydney, deal with the flack and try to discover who did this. Try to clear my reputation and move on.'

'Maybe the network already has. Have you heard from them since you left?'

'No. But I don't have a phone, and I didn't leave any contact numbers. Although Aunt Bea did say the network had called her. I just wish they would leave her alone. She doesn't deserve to be pulled into this mess.' She held his gaze and squeezed his fingers.

'And neither did you. But you know what?' Her pretty lips tilted in a smile.

'What?'

'There's nothing like dumping your problems on a relative stranger to make you feel better. And I am feeling better with each day that passes.'

Chapter 13

The night spent at Top Springs, and the road trip the following day were uneventful. Claire had no more bad dreams, and Don seemed a little bit more aloof since he'd shared his idea of pretending that Claire could pose as his wife. Dinner had been as good as he'd promised, and their conversation had been light, mainly information Don shared about how the charter would work.

There had been no more hand holding, or brushed fingers, and on the way back to the camp site, he had kept a distance between them.

With a brief good night, Don had waited until Claire was in her swag. She'd zipped it up and fallen asleep almost immediately.

Now the sign post ahead said that Wyndham was only a few kilometres ahead.

'Not far off, now,' Don said as he changed back a gear.

Claire nodded and looked at the landscape flashing past. Salt pans that stretched as far as she could see to the west were edged by a low mountain range.

'This is the beginning of the Kimberley,' Don said. 'Spectacular landforms, deep rivers, salt pans and wetlands. And great fishing. Things unique to the north.'

'It's very different. The earthy colours are beautiful,' Claire added.

'Don't be put off when you see Wyndham. The town's had its booms and busts, and since the meatworks closed, tourism is one of the things that keeps it going. It's the only deep-water port between Broome and Darwin, and exports of cattle, nickel, iron ore & produce from the Ord River area do make it a busy little port.'

As they approached the port, she looked with interest at the wide expanse of brown water. 'It's so wide.'

'It's where the King, Pentecost, Durack, Forest and Ord Rivers all meet the sea.' Don laughed. 'Excuse my geography talk. I've used it for the talks I give on the charter.'

Claire frowned as a thought hit her. 'Will I be expected to know about the Kimberleys, do you think? Being your … wife.'

Don shook his head as he turned onto a road that ran along beside the wide brown river. 'No. I'll make it clear that this is your first trip. But I suppose living at Second Chance Bay, you should know a bit about the Gulf.'

'Did I grow up there or did I come there after we got married?'

The look on Don's face was comical and she chuckled. 'This was your idea, so you'll have to get used to it.'

'I know. We'd better get our stories straight.' He pulled up outside a high cyclone fence but kept the engine running as he opened the door. 'Tonight, when we're on the boat,' he said as he climbed out to unlock the gate.

They drove about a hundred metres along the river to a wharf. 'The *Adventurer* is on a floating pontoon at the end,' Don explained. 'To cater for the tidal flow and the wet.'

'This is where the guests get on?' Claire looked around. They'd come through the small township and had crossed through the port, and she hadn't seen any hotels. 'Where do they stay? You said it was an upmarket—'

'An upmarket charter,' Don finished for her. 'Yes, we are. The guests fly to Kununurra and we coach them from there in an air-conditioned coach. Some come in from *El Questro* too. We've got tonight by ourselves, and then the rest of the crew will arrive in the helicopter tomorrow.'

'The helicopter?'

'Yes, that's a heli-pad you'll see on the top deck. We use the helicopter to go to the top of some

170

the waterfalls, and for sightseeing. Then one day to get organised and the guests arrive in time for cocktails.'

'Who flies the helicopter?'

'Not me. I hate flying. We have our own pilot on board. Again, it's a new guy this charter. If you're lucky, he might give you a hand with the serving and clearing up. The last pilot was a great help. He hated sitting around doing nothing and pitched in to help wherever he could.'

A shaky feeling ran from Claire's stomach to her throat as nerves hit again. It was getting very real, and very close.

'Um, you said cocktails? Will I be expected to make them?'

'You will. But don't worry it's easy to learn. If you can follow a recipe, you can make a cocktail.'

'I hope so.'

Don's laughter was warm. 'Claire, stop worrying. You'll be fine. I wouldn't have asked you to do this if I'd thought you weren't up to it.'

'Can we have a practice?'

'We can. We'll work out a past for you tonight and I'll teach you how to make cocktails. But don't worry. It's a set menu for dinner and cocktails the first night. My special "Top Ender" cocktail, and then the guests usually move to wine.'

He parked the ute in a parking bay next to a small shed at the wharf. 'Here we are.'

Claire widened her eyes. She's known it was a luxury charter, but she hadn't expected a boat anywhere near the size of this one.

She stepped out of the ute and put her hand to her eyes. A sleek white hull, at least thirty metres long, and with three decks reaching high, was moored at the wharf. The boat gleamed in the hot northern sun, and oozed luxury … and money.

Don unlocked the door of the shed. 'I store the swags and camping gear in here, so leave your bags over there. I'll get this away and then we'll board.' He quickly unpacked the ute and then carried a small ladder over to the side of the boat.

'I was wondering how we get up there.' Claire pointed to the opening at the back of the deck.

'I'll climb onboard and then drop the gangway for you. It needs to stay down because the first food deliveries will be here late this afternoon.'

A few minutes later, he was up the ladder and unlatched a half-door that Claire hadn't noticed in the side of the deck. The steel gangway slid to the wharf with a clang, and Don came down and after he'd secured it, he picked up her suitcase.

'Ready to come aboard, Mrs McDougal?'

She nodded. 'The guests will call me Claire, I hope, because I'd never remember to answer to that.'

Once on board the boat, it was obvious that the vessel had been restored meticulously. Don had said on the trip across that he'd worked on it over a couple of years, and the boat was in top condition. The rails had been polished to a high gleam, and once they were inside the huge saloon on the middle deck where the gangway had been lowered from, it was obvious that he had fitted it out with quality inclusions.

'Welcome to my *Adventurer*. It'll good to be back on board. I miss her when I'm over at the Bay.'

Claire took a breath and let it out slowly. 'Wow. This is just amazing.'

'Come with me, and I'll show you the cabins up near the wheelhouse. You can leave your stuff up there safely.'

Claire followed him up a set of polished timber stairs. 'Do you have a safe on board?'

He nodded. 'There's a safe in each cabin, and I've got one in my suite. Why do you ask?'

She patted her handbag with a wry grin. 'I've got a fair bit of cash in my bag, and it will be good to put it somewhere safe for the trip.'

'Sure.' He grinned. 'I've noticed you were very attached to it.'

She pulled a face. 'I don't have any of my credit cards with me. I was trying to stay incognito.'

At the top of the stairs, there were two doors and a narrow corridor leading to a huge well-lit space. 'That's the wheelhouse, and the door on the left is my cabin and the other is the spare, where the hostess usually stays.'

Claire wondered why the hostess had a cabin up here when the rest of the crew were elsewhere, but she pushed away the suspicion that jumped into her mind.

Don pushed open the door of the second cabin and put her suitcase inside. 'If you want to leave your bag in there while I show you around up here it'll be safe.' She went to follow him in, but he put the case down and stepped back before she was expecting it. She was wedged in a narrow space between Don and the door.

'Sorry.' He was so close his breath was warm on her lips, and Claire fought the desire to reach out and hold his arms.

Get over it, she thought. *It's only because he's been kind.*

They did a sort of step left, step right and then they were both back in the corridor and there was space between them again.

174

He led her to the wheelhouse and pointed to the array of computerised nautical stuff on a wide bench that ran along a wide glass windscreen with a three-sixty view over the water. 'This is where I'll spend most of my time.'

Claire stepped into the large space. There was a door on each side that led out onto a narrow deck that appeared to run the length of the boat on each side. Don looked around as he crossed over to the bench and flicked some switches. 'We're still on land power, so I'll run the air to cool the boat down a bit.' He picked up a folder with a glossy blue cover and handed it to her. 'This might help you understand your role over the next ten days. There's a map of the boat and a guide to where everything is stored too; linen and all that sort of stuff. It's Jenni's work. She said it would make it a lot easier for the staff when they were learning their way around the boat.'

'Thank you.' She took the folder from him. Already, she was feeling a distance between them. Rather than being her transport—and new friend— as he had been the past couple of days as they'd travelled forty-eight hours, Don was now the captain, and as such, her boss.

'So we've got some work to do today. But you've got two days to learn your way around and get the cabins ready for the guests.'

'Okay. I'll sit down and read it. It'll be good to get to work.'

'Great. I've got some calls to make, but first thing I think you should do is get to know the boat. While I make my calls, have a good look around. Explore the whole boat. In the cabins, the storage areas, and in the galley. Best way to get a feel for the *Adventurer*.'

He led her back downstairs and took her to the main saloon. 'Have a read of Jenni's guide, and when you're ready, have a wander around. I'll be on board most of the time if you've got any questions, but I've got to go up to the port office for a while now. Make yourself at home. There's plenty of water and cold drinks in the cool room, and there's a coffee machine over there.'

'Don?'

He paused and looked at her.

'I'm fine. You don't have to worry. You go and do whatever you have to, and I'll have a read of the manual and get my bearings.'

'Thanks, Claire. You're a champion. You still don't realise how much you've got me out of a fix.'

'Go. I'm sure you've got a lot to do!'

'Yes, ma'am.' He stopped in the doorway and his grin was cheeky. 'Keep that up, and no one will be in any doubt who the boss is.

Chapter 14

Sunset over the Cambridge Gulf—as Claire now knew it was called after reading the staff manual—was spectacular. The salt flats across the river glistened like diamonds and the hues of the sandstone cliffs behind them deepened to reds, oranges and golden brown. Not only did Claire now know the name of the gulf, but she also knew what every storage area on the boat held, where the washing machines and dryers were located on the back of the top deck near the entry down to the cramped cabins of the crew, and where the charter was going. She'd unpacked her suitcase in her cabin and hung up the shirts for her uniform.

She also knew the role of each crew member, and the itinerary for the charter. She'd memorised a bit about each location, so she could sound knowledgeable for the guests. If there was one thing she had, it was a good memory As Don had said, the guests would board for cocktails the day after tomorrow, and then they would depart at approximately six-thirty. Dinner would be served shortly after leaving port and then they would cruise overnight to the King George River.

That's when her work would begin. Until she got over the hurdle of meeting the guests, her nerves were on a fine edge. Keeping herself busy all afternoon had stopped her dwelling on the possibility of being recognised.

With a sigh, she watched as the sun slipped below the horizon in a stunning display of colours.

'I never get tired of the brilliant colours up here.'

Claire jumped when Don spoke. 'I thought you were still down on the wharf.' A delivery truck had been unloading up the gangway for the past hour, so she'd settled herself on the other side of the boat to stay out of the way.

'All done. Food's on board, and the alcohol. The cool room is chockers. Steve, the new chef, has done a great job with the menus and the orders. All I have to see now is that he can actually cook! Are you ready for a cocktail-making lesson?'

'I am.' She stood, and Don stepped back to let her go down the stairs in front of him.

'You've learned your way around,' he said as she led him to the bar at the back of the saloon on the upper deck.

'I have, and I know this is where the first night cocktails are served before we head to King

George River and wait for the tide to rise so we can cross the sand bar.'

'I'm impressed.' His eyes crinkled as he grinned at her, and those damn nerves in her stomach skittered all over again.

'And I also know that the cocktail we're about to make is called a "Top Ender".'

'Like I said, you're a quick learner.'

Claire smiled ruefully. 'You'd be surprised what I had to learn in my job, and how fast I had to absorb it.' She pointed to the bar stool. 'Sit down, Captain, and I'll make your welcome cocktail.'

Don shook his head with a big grin and sat on the chrome and black leather swivel stool.

***

Claire was smiling, and she looked more relaxed than he'd seen her, even though she was about to start charter work that was going to be arduous. Her blue eyes sparkled as she mixed the rum, pineapple juice, squeezed the limes and chopped the mint that he'd unpacked and stowed in the cool room on the bottom deck mid-afternoon. She'd been busy; he hadn't even seen her in the cool room, but she must have scoped out the delivery when they'd finished.

With a flourish of her hand, she decorated the top of the cocktail with a sugared mint leaf on top of the shaved ice and handed it to him. 'Welcome aboard. I hope you enjoy your charter on the *Kimberley Adventurer*, sir.'

Don held her gaze as he lifted the glass to his lips and sipped. Without breaking eye contact he leaned forward and slid another glass over. Claire's cheeks were flushed when he finally looked away to pour half of his cocktail into the second glass. He passed it to her, and then lifted his glass to clink on the side of hers. 'Cheers and welcome aboard to you, too.'

She lowered her eyes as she sipped, but the flush high on her cheeks stayed there. 'Thank you.'

Don slid off the stool and carried his drink across to the sofa under the window that looked out over the back deck. A jacuzzi spa was set at the far end. 'Come and sit where it's comfortable. It's probably the last chance we'll get to sit down for the next ten days.'

'The *Adventurer* is an absolute credit to you, Don,' Claire said softly as she sat beside him.

'Thank you. I'm pretty proud of her.' He sat back and closed his eyes. The long drive and the manual work this afternoon—not to mention the potent effect of a rum cocktail—had him fighting a yawn. He put his glass on the table in front of them. 'Now we have some work to do. But first, any questions or concerns you have about your role?'

Claire shook her head. 'I think I've got it all sorted.'

'I'll get one of the deckies to give you a hand with the cabins tomorrow.'

'I've already done them.'

'No, I mean with making up the beds and putting the towels and toiletries in there.'

'I've already done them. I found the list of names and which cabins they were allocated to, so I've already made them up. But I would like you to check that they're okay.'

Don stared at her. 'You're a wonder. But be careful.'

He regretted his teasing words as soon as her face fell.

'Be careful? Did I do something I shouldn't have?'

'No.' He reached out and took her hand in his. It was good to feel the soft warmth of her skin against his again. 'I meant if you work that fast, you'll have a job for life.'

He was rewarded with a wide smile, and her hand stayed where it was.

'All we have to do now is get our stories straight and invent a past,' she said.

He nodded. 'How about another cocktail, and some nibbles to go with it?'

'Is that wise?'

181

He squeezed her fingers. 'A wine or a soft drink instead if you're worried about a headache.'

'Oh, what the heck,' she said. 'If we're going to be so busy let's live dangerously.'

After the third cocktail, Don was feeling mellow—and hungry. They'd worked on a simple story. Claire was from Gilgandra in outback New South Wales—she knew the area where Aunt Bea had lived—and had met Don on a working holiday in the Gulf. They'd known each other for twelve months, had a whirlwind courtship, moved in together and married last winter. The hostessing story was what he'd suggested—she missed him too much, and they were going to live on the boat for the wet season.

A couple of hours later Claire put her empty glass on the table and giggled. 'I'm starving, Captain. Is there anything to eat?'

'How about some fresh prawns? If we only have a few each, the chef won't notice that the order is a bit light on.' He winked at her.

Gawd, he'd winked at her, like some sleaze.

'You're the boss, aren't you?' She winked back at him and then sat up straight.

And she winked back.

Damn the woman, Don knew when he was in trouble.

'Is there any fresh bread or did you freeze it all?' Her words were clear but the little hiccup that escaped from her lips made him smile.

'Come on.' He stood and put his hands out to Claire and pulled her up. She came up faster than he'd expected and before he could step back, her soft curves pushed up against his chest as she looked up at him.

'Woops, sorry. I forgot the rule.' Her breath warmed his lips.

'What rule?' he whispered.

'Um, wasn't there one about the captain and the crew?' Her lips seemed to be closer as he held her gaze. Her eyes were shining up at him, and a smile played about those pretty lips.

He sighed. 'I don't remember. Did I say there was?'

'I distinctly remember you saying there wasn't to be any freter ... and frater ... oh you know what you meant.'

'Fraternisation?'

'Ye—' But the word was cut off as their lips met and clung. Don closed his eyes. He wasn't sure who'd closed the distance, but all he knew was that he was happy right where he was at that moment. The first time he'd kissed Claire it had been driven by sympathy; this time it had nothing to do with feeling sorry for her. It wasn't about anything apart from how much he wanted to hold her, to feel her lips against his.

He stopped thinking when Claire's lips opened slightly. She tasted of rum, and sunshine, and tropical islands. He could almost hear the music playing, and the palm trees rustling. Lowering one hand he slowly pulled her closer. She eased in against him, fitting as though she was made for him. A small sigh escaped her lips and he gently teased her lips with his tongue. Her arms wound around his neck and her soft curves pressed closer.

'Are you sure you want to eat?' he murmured against her lips.

'I ... I'm—' She stiffened in his arms and pulled back a little. He opened his eyes as a voice called from the deck.

'Ahoy there. Is there anyone on board?'

Claire's eyes were wide as she stepped back, and her cheeks flushed. She put her hand to her lips and then smoothed her hair. Don tried to focus his thoughts as footsteps clattered up the gangway.

'Gidday.' A tall gangly guy with red hair stood in the doorway of the saloon. 'I saw the light on, so I thought I might be able to doss here tonight.' His accent was Scottish.

Don narrowed his eyes. 'How did you get through the gate?'

'I climbed over the fence. My gear's on the other side.' He walked in and held out his hand, shooting a curious look in Claire's direction, and Don bristled. 'I'm Steve Smyth. Your chef.'

'Ah.' Don blinked and held out his hand as realisation kicked in. 'Sorry, Steve, you threw me there for a minute. You can't be too careful. I'm Don McDougal, the skipper.' He glanced at Claire. 'And this is … my wife, Claire.'

'Sorry I'm late. I got held up—not literally—I mean I had bike troubles at Halls Creek, and I was late getting away this morning. I couldn't raise anyone at the caravan park up the road, so I was going to kip in a paddock, and then I thought I'd see if there was anyone on the boat. I thanked my lucky stars when I saw your ute there, and the lights on.'

Don wondered what else he'd seen from the wharf, and then realised that he'd just introduced Claire as his wife, so it didn't matter. He shook Steve's hand and looked at Claire again. 'We were … ah … just about to cook some dinner.' He shot an apologetic glance at Claire. 'Sweetie'—the word felt strange as it came out— 'would you put the kettle on and maybe rustle us up some toast.'

The look directed his way was hard to read, but her words were even. 'Sure, darling. Nice to meet you, Steve.'

'You too, Claire. Is there anyone else on board yet?'

'No, the rest of the crew will be here tomorrow lunchtime. I'll unlock the gate for you. If you want, you can lock your bike in the shed too.'

'Awesome.' Steve the chef beamed at both of them.

Claire headed towards the galley. Don frowned. Her voice was terse, and she didn't look back. 'I'm not hungry. I'll put the kettle on, and slice some bread, and then I'll go to bed. It's been a long day. Good night.'

'Ah, okay. I'll get Steve settled in the crew's quarters, and then I'll be up once I secure the boat.'

She looked down as she walked past him, and Don stopped the groan that threatened to come from his mouth.

Something was wrong.

Chapter 15

Claire couldn't believe what had happened—or what had almost happened—in the saloon. Anger nudged rational thinking aside.

Pretend to be my wife? he'd said.

Pah! All along, Don had been playing Mr Nice Guy, with the goal of getting her into bed. She'd been a fool to fall for it. Three drinks and all her self-protection had gone out the window.

So badly damaged by what had happened, Claire knew she'd given her trust too quickly, and way too easily. Not only had Don McDougal got a hostess on the cheap—and he was probably paying below award rates—he thought he'd got a bed partner for the duration of the trip. No matter what he'd said about doing the right thing.

Stupid, stupid, stupid. He'd been playing her the whole time and she'd fallen for it. Show a bit of sympathy, share a gentle kiss, pull back and show more kindness. And then ply her with rum, and she'd been putty in his hands.

The worst part was, she'd wanted to go to his bed. Almost since the minute she'd met him.

187

She'd never been attracted to a man like that before. Ever.

Fast and furious. A casual physical attraction. In different circumstances it might have been different. But as he'd said, he was her boss, and there'd be no relationship on board.

Not if she had anything to do with it.

As the effects of the three rum cocktails began to wear off, a headache began to niggle at her temples in a consistent rhythm. Apart from the nibbles that Don had dug out of the cool room she hadn't eaten a proper meal all day, nor had she drunk enough water. She wrenched the tap on, and filled the kettle and sliced some thick, jagged edged pieces of bread, and put them on a plate next to the toaster. She opened the cool room and reached for one of the bottles of water she'd seen there earlier.

Don and Steve were down on the wharf and she watched them for a moment before she closed her eyes and rolled the cool bottle on her forehead. Claire knew she wanted more than Don was offering. His kiss had held a promise; he'd set her head spinning with that long intimate touch of his lips on hers, and the way his hand had caressed her had left her with an unfulfilled ache. She sighed.

At the moment, she couldn't think clearly enough to know what she wanted.

But one thing was certain, she didn't need any more complications in her life. Ten days on the boat—it was too late to change her mind about masquerading as Don's wife. She'd already been introduced to the chef as the skipper's wife.

'Sweetie!' he'd said. *She'd give him sweetie.*

With her head thudding with pain, and her mind spinning with thoughts of how much Don had disappointed her, she pushed open the door of her cabin, pleased that she'd made her bed up earlier. Slipping out of her dress, she kicked off the white-soled shoes she'd worn all day and lay back on the bed.

Claire dozed lightly for a short while until there was a soft tap on the door.

She rolled over and buried her face in the pillow. If she ignored him, he'd go away. She lay there holding her breath and sat up with a gasp as the door opened a little way and a chink of light shone on her face.

'Claire?' Don's voice was soft.

'Go away. I'm asleep. Or I was.'

'I want to talk to you. I want to apologise.'

The last thing Claire wanted was a fake apology; he must think she was a soft touch. 'Okay, apology accepted.'

She blinked as the cabin light came on and Don stepped into her cabin, shutting the door behind him.

'Do you mind? I am entitled to some privacy, and I believe this is my cabin?'

'I was worried you might be upset.'

'About what? Twigging to what you're really up to?

'What?'

'You know what I mean. I'm still here, aren't I?' She kept her eyes level with his. Pride helped her speak casually.

A muscle ticked in his jaw and she knew he wasn't as calm as he was making out. 'I promised to help you out with your problem, and I'm a man of my word.'

She rolled over and turned her back to him. 'Please turn the light off on your way out before you shut the door.'

The door closed with a loud click and she brushed away the first tear that rolled down her cheek.

***

Don was too angry to go to bed, and he headed into the wheelhouse. He and Steve had eaten a sandwich—prawns—and had a coffee, and Steve had apologised.

'I'm sorry, skipper. I'm knackered, I'm going to have to hit the sack.'

Don had shown him the cabin in the crew's quarters. And yes, as Claire had said, the beds were made up and there were fresh towels in the bathrooms.

What the hell was Claire playing at? He'd had no intention of kissing her, until she came onto him, and then he couldn't resist those soft lips. He'd made it quite clear where he'd stood all along, but she'd crumbled his defences.

And the rum hadn't helped.

Who knows where they'd be now if Steve hadn't arrived.

In bed in his cabin; he had no doubt of that.

Just as well that Steve had arrived when he had, and she'd chucked a hissy fit.

Let that be a lesson to you, he told himself.

Women and work do not mix.

##

Just as well Steve was a chatterbox. The mood between Claire and Don was as distant when they both arrived in the galley at the same time the next morning. He stood back and gestured to the door. She stopped in the corridor.

'After you,' he said.

Claire put her head down and went straight to the cool room and pulled out a bottle of water. Steve's cheery whistle preceded him along the corridor, and he walked into the galley with a smile as Don was filling the kettle.

'Leave that with me, skipper. I'll get some breakfast going for you. Nice set-up you've got here.'

Don nodded. 'Thanks. That'd be great. We've got a bit to do today.' He turned to Claire. 'Although you're pretty much on top of things, aren't you, love?'

'I am. But I'm sure I can find something to do.' She turned to Steve and the smile she bestowed on him had Don narrowing his eyes as jealousy surged through him.

Bloody hell. He didn't need that.

'I can give you a hand down here, Steve. I've done all the cabins,' she said.

'Sweet, that'd be great. I want to rearrange the pantry and check off the order to make sure I've got everything I need before we leave port. I haven't been to Wyndham before, there's not a lot here. Any shops?'

Don nodded. 'There's a grocery store back in the first bit of town. Before you get to the port. Claire, if Steve needs anything, take the ute out of the shed. The keys are on the shelf in *our* cabin.'

'I will.' Her cheeks flushed, and he felt mean.

'What would you like for breakfast, you pair?' Steve poked his head into the cool room. 'How about an omelette?'

'I'm fine, thanks. I'll just grab a piece of toast later, and a coffee from the machine in the bar,' Claire said. 'I'll be back down to help you in half an hour.'

She put her head down as she walked past Don and didn't meet his eye. He was still feeling cross with her and wanted to sort it out before the crew and passengers arrived and they embarked on the charter.

'Thanks, Steve. I'll come back down in half an hour too. An omelette sounds good.' He turned to the door and hurried after Claire.

'Wait up, Claire. I'll come up with you,' he called after her as she headed for the staircase leading up to the top deck. Her back was rigid as he followed her up the stairs and she pushed open the door to her cabin. 'You'd better get used to going into *our* cabin before the crew are wandering around, if you want to stay as Claire McDougal.' His voice was harder than he'd intended but he was still smarting from the smile that Claire had given Steve. 'And maybe less flirting with the chef would make being my wife more believable.'

She swung around and stared at him, two spots of colour on her cheek. 'What did you say?'

'You heard me.'

Claire folded her arms and stared at him. 'What is your problem?'

Don ran his hand through his hair. 'No, Claire. You're the one with the problem. All of a sudden, I'm the big baddie. Okay, so we had a few drinks and I let my guard down, but remember it was a two-way street. You kissed me too.'

She put her head down, and he could see her lip quivering, but he didn't soften. 'However you feel about me—and you're sending mixed messages—we need to sort this out before everyone else arrives. Two things: no one's going to believe our story, and second, I don't want disharmony on the boat. You can feel what you feel, but keep it hidden. If you can't you can get off now, and somehow I'll manage.'

Her head lifted and he almost broke when he saw her eyes awash with tears.

***

'I'm sorry.' Claire kept her voice steady, even though she felt awful. 'I was in the wrong, and the way I spoke to you was unacceptable. I'll be polite from now on.'

Don shook his head and reached out, putting his hand on her shoulder as she stared at him. 'I don't want polite, Claire. And if you treat me distantly, it'll be as obvious as—'

'I said I was sorry. What I said was awful.' She shifted her gaze from his. 'It's no excuse, but at the moment I've forgotten how to trust anyone. I thought about everything you said, and I know I thought the wrong thing.'

'And what was that?' His piercing gaze pinned her.

'I guess I thought that all you wanted was a bed partner for the trip. I guess I wondered why the hostess cabin was up here.'

He laughed but it held no mirth. 'That's the way the cabins were when I bought the boat. Would you really like to be down in the crew's quarters sharing the bathroom with five blokes?'

'No.'

'And Claire, this isn't over between us by a long shot. But if you think I was only after sex, maybe you don't know me well enough. But I think we should call a truce and talk about this after the trip. What do you think?'

When he smiled at her, Claire managed to smile back. 'Okay,' she said softly. 'And please say you accept my apology?'

She was supposed to be an intelligent woman, but she'd let her emotions get the better of her, acting more like an insecure teenager.

'Of course, I do. I know what you've been going through, and I'm sure you're nervous about everyone coming on board.'

'I am. Almost sick to the stomach.' She took a deep breath. 'But with your support, I'll get through it.'

She looked at the hand he held out to her and was sorely tempted to take it. To go back to where they'd been last night, but she shook her head. 'I've got one small job to do'—she ran her hand along the top of her hair—' and then I'll be down.'

His brow wrinkled in a frown, and she pointed to her head again.

'My hair. I don't want a hint of dark roots growing through in the next ten days. Just in case anyone is suspicious.'

Don chuckled. 'Fair enough. How long will that take? I'll save you some omelette. You need to eat, no matter how nervous you are.'

'Thanks. I'll be down in half an hour.' Claire reached out and touched his cheek. Don hadn't shaved and the stubble on his skin sent a small quiver shooting down her tummy. 'I'll see you down there.'

Chapter 16

The mood on the *Adventurer* the next night was jovial … for most of the crew.

So far so good.

Sean, Haydn, and Travis, the three deckhands, were all in their early twenties and hadn't batted an eyelid or shown any interest when Don had introduced Claire as his wife, and the charter hostess.

Derek, the helicopter pilot, a man in his mid-forties, with tanned and weathered skin, had looked at her curiously, and Claire's breath had caught. Eventually he'd looked away and made a comment to Don about it being a better boat than any he'd been on. They'd arrived in the helicopter, and it was now secured on the helipad. Uniforms had been issued, but the crew were in civvies tonight.

Don called a meeting for the whole crew before dinner, once they'd settled in and checked out the boat. Claire sat on the sofa at the back of the timber-lined saloon where she and Don had drunk rum cocktails last night.

Was it only last night? It seemed longer.

'Welcome aboard, everyone. It's good to have you here. Beers are on me tonight, but as soon as the guests are on board, we have a no drinking rule until the end of the charter. I hope the agency told you about that. I run a tight ship, and I'd appreciate you letting me know of any problems as soon as they happen.'

They all nodded, but Derek didn't look too impressed. Claire thought she was the only one who caught Derek's eye roll when Don turned back to the small bar fridge.

'Any questions, please hit me with them now. We're going to be busy from tomorrow afternoon,' Don said.

Sean looked around and then put his hand up.

Don smiled. 'No need for a hand, mate. What do you want to know?'

Claire had already noticed that Sean was the quiet and serious one of the three "deckies" as they called themselves. It was a whole new world for her.

'What route are we taking, skipper?'

'King George River, the Drysdale, a heli-picnic at Toe River will keep you busy on the third day, Derek, and then the three of you will be full on with the fishing at the back end of the charter. We'll go across to Mitchell River and Surveyor's Creek.'

Steve grinned. 'One day I'll be rich enough to go on one of these trips as a guest.' He laughed and nudged Derek. 'Only problem is the meals wouldn't be as good as what I'd do.'

Derek looked back at him with his lip curled and Claire decided she didn't like him in that moment.

'Got tickets on yourself, mate?' he said.

'Nah, I'm just the best chef around up here these days. You can tell me what you think at the end of the trip.'

A good comeback, Claire thought. She caught Don's eye and he held her gaze, and they shared a moment of understanding. He'd picked Derek as a problem too. She hadn't realised how hard it would be getting an agency to organise staff that you were in close quarters with for the length of a charter.

'Good to hear, Steve. So far what you've produced has been great.' Don handed over the cans of beer he'd pulled out of the fridge.

When he went to hand one to Derek, the older man said curtly, 'I'd rather have spirits.'

Don raised his eyebrows as Derek crossed to the bar and took down a bottle of top shelf whiskey.

'Okay, seeing it's the first night, sprits are fine.' He and Claire exchanged another look.

199

The conversation was social as they sat around the saloon. Steve finished his beer and went to cook, and Derek left with a sullen look when Don screwed the cap on the bottle and put the whiskey back on the top shelf.

The three young deckies laughed and joked as the aroma of pizza wafted through the saloon. Rather than messing up the dining room, they all moved out to the deck to eat, when Steve called out that the pizzas were ready.

Derek came back up and looked curiously at Claire as he reached for a slice of pizza. 'You ever worked in Darwin?'

She shook her head as her stomach tightened. 'No, why?'

'Thought I knew you from one of the other boats, or somewhere.' He narrowed his eyes, and Claire forced a cheerful note into her voice.

'Not me. I've never been to Darwin. What about you, have you been to Karumba? Maybe you've seen me there in the fish co-op. I help the family out when we're home.' She crossed her fingers behind her back. The first of the lies didn't come easily.

'Nah, never been there. You must look like someone I know.' He wiped his mouth with the back of his hand.

A real charmer.

'They say we all have a *doppelganger,* don't they?'

Don met her gaze and smiled. They'd had this conversation before he'd known who she was.

'A doppel what?' Derek said gruffly.

'A *doppelganger* is the German for "double walker",' Sean said. 'It means a person who looks incredibly similar to you.'

'Yeah, I knew that,' Derek said.

As they cleaned up after dinner, he disappeared leaving his plate out on the deck. Claire didn't hold any hope for Derek helping her with the meals when there were eighteen guests to look after.

***

Don followed Claire up the stairs after she'd cleaned the saloon and helped Steve in the galley. Even though she and Don had made their peace, she still felt uncomfortable around him, mainly because of the attraction she felt. Seeing him work today, and how good he was with the crew, and how deftly he'd handled Derek, just added to it.

Tonight, she'd moved her things into the master cabin in case anyone was poking around. She didn't trust Derek; a few times Claire had caught him looking at her, and she didn't like the thoughtful expression on his face.

'Got a minute, Claire?' Don's voice was polite, as it always was now. She was pleased that he'd talked to the crew in his introduction about professional behaviour at all times, because it let them keep a distance between each other that was professional, rather than the affectionate touching of a couple.

'Yes, sure.' She hid the nervous tone in her voice, as she wondered whether he was coming to bed now.

He closed the door behind them and crossed to the large window that looked over the water to the mountains. It was late, and a few scattered lights of distant houses blinked in the darkness. Claire sat on the small chair that was in the corner of the cabin.

'What do you think of Derek?' he asked.

'He could be difficult, I guess.' Claire put her elbow on her knee and propped her chin in her hand. 'I guess it depends what he's like with the guests. He's a bit gruff.'

Don sighed and leaned against the wall. He looked tired and a wave of feeling rushed through Claire. 'He came highly recommended, but I think I might have been dudded with a less than honest reference. It happens up here. The less than scrupulous operators often pass on staff who don't work out like that. But a good pilot is scarce up here. They get snapped up.'

'It's too late to replace him now, isn't it?'

Don's hair stood up in untidy spikes when he rubbed at it. 'Yes, it is. I'll just have to keep a close eye on him. And I'm sorry, I don't think he's the kind to help you out when it gets busy.'

'I've already picked that. But don't worry. Steve's great, and it'll work out.' Claire pointed to the bed. 'You look really tired. Why don't you get some sleep? I'll take the small bed.'

'Thanks. This will be the last night that I'm in here. I'll be in the wheelhouse and on watch once we're underway.'

'All night?'

'Four hours on, and four hours off, but until I know that the deckies can do a proper watch, I'll stay in there with them.' He crossed the room and sat on the side of the bed and toed his shoes off. 'How are you feeling about tomorrow? Nervous?'

'Surprisingly, no.' And she was telling the truth. She was more nervous being around Don than with the thought of the guests arriving. 'The thing with Derek, it let me practise what I'd say if it comes up. They all seem to have accepted we're married without a problem.'

'They've got no reason to question it.' Don yawned and lay back on the pillow. Within minutes he was asleep. Claire had intended reading the book she'd taken from the guest bookshelf, but now that

Don was out like a light, she let her gaze linger on his face.

Chapter 17

As the afternoon grew later, Claire's nerves were in a jumble. Steve's normal happy-go-lucky mood had snapped when she'd dropped the third cup on the galley floor and it had broken.

'Shit, Claire, go and polish the windows or summat.' His Scottish accent broadened when he was upset. Everyone was on edge as they waited for the coach with the guests to arrive. Don had taken her through the guest list last night when he'd woken up, and there were only a couple from Sydney that she thought may know the program. But it was all an unknown. In the end she calmed down, telling herself that worrying wouldn't change anything.

She hovered around the bar, polishing glasses—albeit carefully—and checked the bar fridge for the hors d'oeuvres that she'd brought out from the cool room. Steve said he'd have the hot food ready at five o'clock when the guests boarded. She had half an hour to change into her uniform, tidy her hair and put some lipstick—and her clear glass spectacles—on.

Don was in the wheelhouse and she poked her head around the door. 'I'm just going into the cabin to get changed. Is there anything you need?'

Her eyes widened as he turned. He had changed into navy shorts and a white collared polo shirt and a captain's hat sat on his head. His face was cleanshaven, and his hair was damp from the shower. Claire's heart set up a patter.

'No, all good here. The coach driver just radioed in, they're ahead of schedule. When you get changed can you please tell Steve they're about ten minutes away. I've let the crew know.'

'Ooh, I'd better get my skates on.'

'Are you okay, Claire?' Don's voice was low as he pointed to the window.

Claire stood on her tiptoes and pulled a face. Derek was sitting at the front of the boat under the windscreen. She leaned close to Don's ear and a waft of woody aftershave tickled her nose. 'Eavesdropping?'

He nodded.

'Okay, sweetheart,' she said loudly. 'We're all good to go in the bar. The cold food's in the fridge, the cocktail prep is done. Let's toast a successful trip when you come down to meet them.'

'Thanks. I'll meet you down there.'

Claire ran lightly down the stairs before she got changed. 'They're early, Steve. Ten minutes.'

'Rightio. I'll be ready. Thanks, luv.'

As she turned to go back upstairs, she came face to face with Derek. His face was sullen, and she stared at him. 'Is anything wrong?'

'Nothing that will concern you.' His mouth was set in a straight line.

She frowned. 'If there is a problem, you'd better tell the … you'd better tell my husband.' The words gave her a funny feeling as they came from her lips.

'Not worth it. He's already had his say.'

Claire looked after him as he slouched away, and then hurried upstairs to get changed.

***

Don looked with pride at his crew standing in a row along the wharf at the base of the gangplank. Even though they were a new crew, they'd all co-operated. Hair was slicked back, and each one was in uniform and wearing the *Kimberley Adventurer* cap—even Claire.

Derek had even done the right thing and was standing at the far end of the row, not looking as morose as usual. Don let his gaze linger on Claire as he waited for the passengers to disembark the coach. He could tell by the set of her shoulders and her hands clenched by her sides that she was really nervous. But as soon as the coach doors opened, and the passengers began to walk across the wharf, a wide smile settled on her face.

Don stepped to the head of the queue and beckoned Claire to come up and stand beside him. The coach driver and his helper directed the passengers over to the gangway before they unloaded the luggage. This was the slowest part of the whole routine. As usual the passengers were excited and wanted to chat and exclaim about the boat—that always filled him with pride—but Don briefly introduced himself to each of the eighteen passengers, before he turned to Claire, saying, 'and this is my wife, Claire. She'll be your hostess for the next ten days.' He held her elbow gently as she stood beside him, and for a moment he could almost pretend what he was saying was true.

Finally, the last of the passengers were onboard, and Claire ushered them to the bar on the middle deck as Sean and Travis carried the luggage to the cabins. By the time Don reached the bar behind the stragglers, Claire already had a tray of cocktails made.

So far no one had appeared to pay undue attention to her, but she kept her eyes down as she mixed the cocktails. The passengers were pretty much as he'd anticipated from the manifest. Five middle-aged couples travelling together from the UK, two elderly couples from rural Queensland,

and the four he had worried about the most: executives from Sydney travelling together with the primary goal of catching fish. They were the most likely to recognise Claire if anyone was going to.

'Welcome aboard. I'll be back to chat in a while,' he said to each couple as he moved through the group as they settled in the bar and out on the back deck, but he had the four guys outside in his sights. Joining the group who already had their cocktails in hand, he took off his hat. 'Welcome aboard guys. You're after fish, I'm told?' Placing his hat on the table at the back of the deck, he held out his hand to each man in turn. I'm Don McDougal, the *Kimberley Adventurer*'s mine and I'm your captain for the charter.'

'Don.' One of the men stepped forward. 'You might not remember me. Jim Smith. I was on your charter out of Karumba six months ago. I had such a great trip, when I saw you had a Kimberley charter, I told the guys we had to come.'

Don looked at him closely. 'Hey Jim! I do remember you. You caught that huge barra the day before we came in. Welcome back.'

'One point three metres.' He almost glowed with pride and his chest puffed out as he held up his hand for a high five. 'You're a secretive bugger. You never mentioned you'd just got married when we were on the trip. Must have been about the same time. When was the wedding?'

Don swallowed. 'Well. You know how it is. I was busy on the boats.'

Jim turned back to the bar. 'You've done well for yourself, mate. Congratulations. Did Claire come to the wharf when we came in on that trip? She looks familiar.'

Don cleared his throat. 'Ah, probably. Anyway, let's hope for some great fishing over the next week. I'll introduce you to Derek, He's going to be taking you guys to some fantastic fishing spots in the helicopter.'

The men all clinked their glasses. 'That's what we're here for.'

Chapter 18

Claire relaxed more as each day passed. The passengers were not a bit interested in her, apart from the meals she delivered, and the clean laundry she delivered to their rooms each day. To be fair, they were a great mix of people, totally focused on relaxation and sightseeing—and in the case of the four men travelling together, catching the biggest, most elusive fish. All the guests were polite and friendly, and not overly curious. She settled into a routine, surprised by how much she was enjoying the charter, now that the risk of anyone recognising her was no longer at the forefront of her mind.

Each day when they went off on an excursion, in the tender or by helicopter to a waterfall or a secret fishing location, they came back happy and hungry.

The job was full on. Claire changed sheets, washed towels, did the guest laundry and cleaned windows and then, three times a day would serve meals to eighteen guests and then cleared the tables when they were done.

Don took over the bar duties at dinner each night, and she was grateful for that.

'But you still have to tally up that bar bill, at the end,' he said with a wink one night. 'That's in your role statement.'

'Thanks, boss,' she said with a smart grin as she wiped down the bar after another busy night. The last guest had gone to bed, and Don and Claire were alone in the bar; the first time she'd been alone with him since the charter had started.

Or as far as she knew she had. Now she looked at him curiously. 'Have you had any sleep at all since we left?'

'I have, but I haven't slept as soundly as you. I was cuddled up close to you last night and you didn't even stir.'

Her head flew up and she gripped the wet sponge. 'You what? What do you mean cuddled up?'

'Sssh. Someone might hear you.'

When she saw the teasing glint in Don's eyes, Claire let fly with the sponge and it hit him square in the chest. Liquid trickled down the front of his shirt, and she giggled when he shivered. But he moved quickly and grabbed her hand and held the sponge over her head with the other one, before she could move.

'Will I squeeze the water out or not?' he wondered aloud.

'Don't even think about it. It's stale beer not water.'

Don pulled her close and she was hard up against him. Sheer pleasure ran through Claire. For the first time in weeks, laughter—created by pure happiness—bubbled up from her chest.

'You are going to so pay for that, girl.' His voice was quiet but teasing. Claire stared up at him, and there was a moment when it was just them, lost in each other's eyes. His head came closer and she put her hand on his chest—his damp chest. A smile played about her lips, as his mouth came closer to hers.

'Come on, you two. Haven't yous got a perfectly good cabin on the top deck?' Steve yawned and scratched his head. 'I came up to check I turned the gas off.'

Claire jumped back, heat suffusing her face and neck, but Don kept his arm loosely around her shoulders. 'Claire has, but I've got to relieve Haydn on watch'—he lifted his arm and put his face near his watch exaggerating the movement so his cheek was pressed against hers— 'in three minutes.'

Claire stepped back as he lifted his arm and she slipped beneath it. 'Well, I still have a load of washing to do and wait to put it in the dryer.' She wrinkled her nose. 'Fishing clothes.'

'Come up to the wheelhouse and talk to me while you wait.' Don ruffled her hair as he headed for the steps. 'I could do with some company.'

The contentment in his voice stayed with Claire as she wiped down the rest of the bar.

Steve walked past her with another yawn. 'See you in the morning, love. I don't know how you do it.'

'Do what?' Claire asked with a frown.

'Look so fresh after a huge day of nonstop work, and you're still going. It must be *lurve*.'

'Go to bed. You're talking rot.' But the smile stayed on her face after Steve headed down to the crew's quarters.

***

Don watched as Claire went back and forward along the deck at the side of the wheelhouse, down to the washing machines and back again.

Despite their worries, the charter had gone well. The crew were competent and cheerful, and even Derek had come around a bit, although Don didn't think he would hire him again. There was just something about him that didn't meld with the rest of the crew. They were halfway through the charter and tomorrow they would be cruising along the

Hunter River, and Derek would take the passengers up to see the Jackson Falls from the air.

Not one person had commented on Claire's likeness to the missing television presenter from Sydney, and he'd seen her relax more as each day had passed.

'Do you want a coffee?' Her face appeared around the door.

'Are you going to have one?' he asked.

'No. I'm going to go to bed.'

'I'm fine. I've got some Coke up here.'

Claire stood in the doorway. 'Okay. I'll get those clothes out early. Are you going to get some sleep tonight?'

'Are you getting lonely in there?' He couldn't help teasing her and smiled when she pulled a face at him.

'Behave, Captain.' She stood in the doorway looking out over the water as the boat cruised silently along the deep waterway.

Don turned the autopilot on before leaving the helm, and walked over to stand beside Claire.

'It's beautiful out here,' she said almost reverently. 'I had no idea how wonderful it is.'

'It certainly gets in your blood.' They stood there silently for a few moments looking up at the diamond bright sky.

'It's like black velvet. As though you could reach out and touch it,' she said.

'You've done really well, Claire.'

'I'm really enjoying myself.'

He hesitated. 'It might sound crazy, but there's a job here for you if you want it next season.'

'Thank you. That's the nicest thing you could have said to me.'

'So?'

She shook her head. 'So, I'll go back to Sydney and sort out my life, and then I'll decide what I'm going to do. I'll probably go back to practising law.'

'I'll miss you.' It felt natural to put his arm around her and Don was pleased when Claire rested her head against his shoulder.

'You could always come down and visit,' she said quietly.

'Is that a real invitation?'

She nodded, and Don smiled. When she looked up at him, her eyes shone in the moonlight; it was hard to see her expression, but still a shaft of need lodged in his soul.

'I'm really going to miss you,' he said.

Claire lifted one hand and cupped his cheek and Don rested his forehead against hers.

'I'll miss … all this, too.'

He pulled back. Disappointment and an emptiness left a hollow ache in his gut. Turning to the helm, he spoke quietly. 'Go to bed, Claire. It's going to be a big day tomorrow.'

But neither of them knew what the day was going to bring.

Chapter 19

The need to tell Don that she didn't want to leave had been hard to ignore. When he'd asked her to stay, Claire had been so tempted, but it wasn't the right thing for her. What the right path for her in life would be, she had yet to discover. This respite—once the fear of being discovered by the media had disappeared when the charter had begun—was simply that. A respite—time to give some thought to her future.

She had to go back and resume her *real* life; this was an interlude, a time to regroup and get her head together. Claire had given a lot of thought to her priorities and working on television was at the very bottom.

And besides, no matter how kind Don was, it was friendship, that was all. The thought of living up here and having a relationship with Don was a dream; he had offered her a job because she had suited his needs on the boat. No more than that, no matter how pleasant it was. She couldn't—wouldn't— give up her life in the city to move permanently to Second Chance Bay.

She rose early and stepped into the bathroom to have a quick shower and put her fresh uniform on. Allowing herself a quick glance into the small alcove beneath the window at the back of the cabin, she could see that Don was asleep, his hands flung high on the pillow. She looked away quickly and ignored the ache in her heart.

She set the breakfast table in the small dining room at the back of the galley where the crew had their meals.

'Morning, Derek,' she said brightly. Even though his demeanour had improved, she still didn't like him as much as the other crew. Steve was a perfectionist, could be terse when he was under pressure at mealtimes, trying to get eighteen entrees and then eighteen mains out for the guests, but she liked him. The three deckhands were happy-go-lucky, but hardworking.

Derek grunted and continued reading without looking at her. As she pulled milk and fruit from the cool room, Steve wandered in rubbing his eyes. 'Pancakes for you lot this morning; you're going to need the energy apparently.'

Sean and Travis wandered in, dressed in their uniforms, ready to start the day; *Haydn must be on watch*, Claire thought, as she put the fruit juice and glasses on the table.

'Thanks, Claire,' Travis said.

Sean looked past her. 'We've already lowered the tender, skipper. I know you want to get an early start.'

Don walked in, his hair damp and a smile on his face. 'Morning all, and thanks Sean. Yep, this is our biggest day. All eighteen have chosen an activity today. Claire I'll get you to go in the tender; there's a swimming hole under the waterfall and four of the guests have opted for that activity.

'Um, crocodiles?' she asked.

Don laughed and shook his head. 'Nope. No crocs there.'

'How many coming with me, Don?' Claire had noticed that Derek never referred to Don as skipper or captain. Derek put the magazine down as Don glanced at the manifest.

'You've got ten today so a few trips up before lunch would be great.'

'I'll take the tender to the swimming hole and then when we get back, Trav is going to take the guys mud-crabbing.' Sean reached over for the magazine that Derek had put down.

Steve brought out a plate loaded with pancakes, but Claire shook her head and reached for the fruit. As she looked up Sean was looking at her curiously. He looked back down at the magazine and then up at her face again.

Claire froze; she looked at the front of the magazine, but slowly let her breath out when she saw it was an old one.

Sean put it flat on the table. 'Has anyone ever told you, you're a dead ringer for that reporter woman.'

Don stiffened across the table from her, but he casually reached across for the magazine. 'Yeah,' he said with an easy smile. 'I told Claire that the first time we saw her on TV on our honeymoon in Sydney. They could be related.'

'Are you, Claire?' Sean persisted.

She shook her head. 'No'—her voice croaked, and she cleared her throat— 'No relation.'

Derek reached across for the magazine. 'That's an old article. She's the one who's gone missing now. 'He narrowed his eyes. 'The network was offering a financial reward for anyone who spotted her.'

Claire laughed, and hoped it didn't sound as artificial as it felt. 'They found her. Don and I saw a picture of her on a beach in France on our way over.' She smiled at Don, but it was a brittle smile. 'Half her luck. This husband of mine took me to Sydney for our honeymoon. I can only dream of the south of France.'

The conversation turned to the best holiday destination, but Claire still felt uncomfortable.

Derek was quiet, and he'd pulled his phone out and was looking at it intently.

Don must have noticed too. He stood as soon as he'd eaten. 'Right, you lot. Time to get to work. Everyone knows the drill for today?'

'Claire?' Steve called out from the galley and she stood and walked in. Tension filled her.

'Yes?' She poked her head around the door.

'There's a basket of cold drinks and morning tea packed. I'll get the boys to put it in the tender for you.'

##

The morning out in the tender was pleasant; the waterhole was crystal clear and cool, and Claire went in for a swim in the pool beneath the waterfall with the English couples.

'Bloody top stuff,' Reg, one of the husbands said as he surfaced after diving in. 'It's going to be hard to go home to snow.'

Claire sat back on a flat rock, shaded by the cliff, giving the guests time to have a long swim before she opened the morning tea basket. Sean had dropped them off and gone back to take the four fishermen to the crabbing creek. There was a two-way radio in the basket if they needed to contact the mothership.

She looked up as Derek flew over in the helicopter. They were so low she could see the delighted expressions on the faces of the guests as they flew over. Twenty minutes later they flew back the other way.

'Morning tea's on, folks.'

She poured out the tropical juice that Steve had packed, and unwrapped the tea towel that held fresh-baked muffins. As she put the plate in the middle of the rock, the loud thudding of a helicopter filled the air. She looked up as a helicopter swooped low over the waterfall; it wasn't the one from the *Adventurer*.

'Busy around here this morning,' Reg commented as he reached for a muffin.

Claire nodded, but was distracted when the radio crackled soon after. The helicopter from the boat passed over again heading west, and she had to walk away to hear what was being said. So much for a quiet morning on the water. There was a huge boab tree about fifty metres away, and she wandered along the edge of the waterhole towards it until the noise of the helicopter had receded.

'Claire, here. Over.'

'Claire, it's Don.'

'What's up?'

His voice was low and urgent. 'There's a bit of a situation here. Sean's coming back to collect the group, but I want you to stay there. Get yourself out of sight as soon as you can. Over.'

223

Claire's blood ran cold. 'What is it? Over.'

'We're about to get visitors. A television network helicopter from Darwin just radioed the boat. I guess it's about you. Shit, I'm sorry, Claire, but I'll deal with it. Just stay out of sight, okay? Over.'

'I will. Over.' Her voice was resigned and, strangely, she accepted the situation. It had only been a matter of time until it came to this.

'Wait there. I'll come and get you when it's safe. Over and out.'

She dropped the two-way to her side and walked back to the group. 'Sean's on his way back,' she said brightly, trying to think of a reason why she wouldn't be going in the tender. 'Um, there's another group coming so I'll stay here and wait for them.'

Sean looked at her curiously when the passengers clambered into the tender and she stepped back. 'You coming, Claire?'

'No. Don's coming out with another group. I'll wait here.'

'Unusual for the skipper to leave the boat.' He gunned the small motor and the front of the tender lifted as they headed down the river. After a few minutes, they rounded a bend and were out of sight.

He was right. Don must be worried if he was leaving the *Adventurer*. Her heart thudding, and her knees trembling, Claire stepped back and looked around. The high cliffs rose majestically above her, and the small waterfall trickled down the rock face to her left. A narrow track led to the top of the cliff, and she headed for it, determined to get out of sight. From up there she would be able to see what was happening on the *Adventurer*. If the helicopter went over again, there were plenty of stands of trees for her to hide in. But she was worried that they'd already probably spotted her as they'd headed towards the boat.

By the time she reached the top, the sound of a helicopter approaching had her looking for cover. She peered through the foliage and let out a sigh of relief; it was Derek and the helicopter from the boat, but still she stayed out of sight until they had passed over.

Claire reached the top of the cliff and looked out to the north, shading her eyes with her hand; the river wound lazily into the distance, but it was very different to the sheltered waterhole below. The *Adventurer* was moored in the middle of the wide channel and another helicopter was hovering above the boat. Even from this distance she could see the spray misting from the churned-up water. She turned back to the river that eventually fell over the cliff and down to the waterhole below. Small rapids tumbled along the rocks upstream.

She drew a sharp breath and froze as something moved in her peripheral vision. Turning her head slowly, her heart pounded, almost in time with the fast-approaching helicopter.

Three large crocodiles were sunning themselves on a flat rock, almost at the top of the waterfall, and only thirty metres away from where she was standing. As she watched, one slid lazily into the water and she backed away silently to the track. Suddenly the thud of the helicopter surrounded her, and she looked up as a man leaned out and pointed at her. The chopper turned and headed for the flat ground next to the waterhole below. Claire had no choice but to go back to the track; the crocodiles were between her and escape.

She bit her lip and prepared for the confrontation that had haunted her for the past month.

Chapter 20

Don quietly briefed Sean when he came back with the guests. Sean's eyes widened as Don headed for the tender.

'You're in charge until I get back,' Don called out. 'Let Steve and the other guys know what's going on, but, mate, if that grey chopper comes back before Derek does, stand on the helipad with one of the others and don't let it land again, okay?'

'Yes, skipper.'

Don jumped in the tender and headed up river. One hand gripped the side of the tender as he pulled the starter cord. His knuckles were white, and he rolled his shoulders, trying to ease the tension.

The situation with the reporters on the media helicopter had been ugly. They'd landed on the boat's helipad without permission, and he'd confronted them.

'What the hell do you think you're doing?' he'd yelled over the noise of the rotors. Finally, they'd stopped and two men in suits had climbed out.

Don had stood with his arms folded and his jaw set. 'I have our chopper about to come in and land, so unless there's an emergency, you need to leave now.'

His worst fear was confirmed, when the taller of the two sauntered over to the deck.

'We're here to interview one of your guests,' he said.

Don played dumb. 'Yes, who? Is there a problem?'

'Sybil Harris.'

Don frowned and shook his head. 'No one of that name on board. You've got the wrong boat, mate.'

The reporter shook his head. 'Nope, this is the one. Maybe you know her as Claire Templeton.'

Don called his bluff and shook his head. 'Nope. Please move that chopper off my boat, I've got one coming in now.' Right on cue, Derek's bird appeared over the cliff face two hundred metres away.

Don had no doubt that it was Derek who'd alerted the media, and they'd turned up bloody quick. At least they couldn't talk to him; while they were on the helipad, he couldn't land.

'We'll be back.' Frustration laced the guy's voice. It looked like he'd thought he had a scoop, or whatever they called it.

They'd climbed back in and taken off immediately and headed upriver. Derek landed the helicopter carrying the guests as soon as they were clear. He avoided Don's eye, as the next guests had climbed into the chopper.

Derek would keep until Claire was safely back on board.

The tender was at top speed as he whizzed up the Roe River towards the swimming waterhole. As he rounded the last bend the grey chopper took off from the clearing.

Shit.

Scanning his surroundings, Don eased back the motor but there was no sign of Claire. He pushed the boat into the small bay and jumped out, quickly securing the anchor to a rock.

'Claire!' Don cupped his hands around his mouth and yelled. The noise of the chopper was fading in the distance, but there was no answer. There was a small opening behind the waterfall. If Claire was hiding in there, she wouldn't be able to see or hear him. Forcing himself to be calm, he clambered over the large rocks and then climbed the five metres up the cliff face.

Even though the waterfall was running at a trickle, the water was cold. Don stepped through the misty curtain.

'Claire!' He looked around the small space as his eyes became accustomed to the darkness, but it was empty.

He ducked through the water again, and back outside, and called again but all was quiet.

Surely those bastards wouldn't have forced her into the helicopter?

Surely she wouldn't have gone with them willingly.

Don stood and stared around him. The landscape was quiet and still.

Claire was gone.

Despair rocked him to the core as he realised how much he cared for her.

In the two weeks since she'd wandered into the courtyard of the store, he'd felt sorry for her, and he'd been sympathetic to her plight. He'd given her a job, and over that time, he'd learned who the real Claire was.

Now he knew what Jenni had meant when she'd told him when he met the right person, he would fall hard and fast.

And he had.

He loved her.

Don pushed himself to his feet, scanning the flat landscape around him before he got back into the small boat. Just as he was about to start the motor he narrowed his eyes; there was a track heading up to the top of the cliff. He hadn't noticed it on previous visits. The gravel crunched beneath his feet as he jumped out of the small boat.

Small rocks tumbled from above as he ran towards the cleared scrub.

'I thought you said there weren't any crocodiles here.'

Relief flooded through him. He stopped and waited as Claire jumped down off the end of the track. 'There's not,' he said. 'They don't body surf down waterfalls.'

'Well, they're up there,' she said. 'And I hope they stay put.' Her voice trembled as she walked over to him.

Don opened his arms and she stepped into them without hesitation.

Thank God. He dropped his head and rested his chin on her hair.

'Why are you here? Why didn't you stay with the boat?' she said.

'Because I needed to make sure you were okay.' His voice was muffled against her cap. 'I couldn't see you. I thought those guys had taken you with them in the helicopter.'

'I'm okay. I hid on the track, but they didn't come after me.' She shook her head. 'I knew they'd seen me coming back down because they turned around and landed down here. I took off when I saw those crocodiles.' Her eyes held his and the smile that spread slowly on her face told him everything he wanted to know. 'I hid behind this huge tree trunk, and stayed put. I know their type; they wouldn't climb up a steep hill like that one. They'll doctor up a photo somehow, now they know I'm here.'

Don watched her face as she smiled up at him. 'I thought I'd lost you, Claire. It was the worst moment of my life.'

'I'm here and you're stuck with me.' Her eyes were shining as they held his. 'Now tell me what you mean exactly by *lost* me?'

***

Claire lifted her face to Don's; the expression on his face was the only thing that mattered to her now. It was more important than any of the situation that had brought her so much stress. But that situation had brought her to Don.

Lost me? She didn't think he was talking about losing a member of the crew. Or she hoped he wasn't.

'I hadn't thought it through.' His arms tightened around her, and happiness settled in her chest. 'I should have known they'd go looking for you. I'm sorry they've found you.'

Her voice was calm as she held his gaze. 'I don't care about them. All that energy I've wasted worrying about being in the news and magazines, it doesn't matter, does it? It's not important.' Claire didn't care anymore about those two journalists—or whoever it was who had spotted her and leaned out with their huge telephoto lens—or what they thought about her. 'I do think they took a photo of me from up there.' The chopper had swooped up the cliff face and hovered over the flat rock where the crocodiles were basking in the sun.

Don cupped her face in his hands and lowered his face to hers. 'So the whole world will know where you are now; how do you feel about that?'

'I don't know that anyone apart from the media will be terribly interested to tell the truth. But I'm *very* happy with where I am right at this moment.'

'So am I.'

Don had left the *Kimberley Adventurer* to make sure *she* was okay. By doing that, he's shown that she was important to him. Claire knew now she'd placed too much importance on the past and the events of the last month. None of that mattered. Don cared for her and he'd put her welfare first. He'd left the boat in someone else's charge and he'd come to find her himself. He could have sent one of the deckhands, but he hadn't and that told her so much.

Don wouldn't let her down, and she hoped it was because he cared for her as she did for him. It was all about trust.

'Thank you.'

'What for?' His voice burred against her cheek.

'For showing me what matters.' Claire lifted her arms and put them around Don's neck and his lips slid slowly along her cheek.

'You're right, Claire. I have to show you …' he said as his mouth moved closer to hers.

She frowned and looked around. 'Show me?'

'How fast … and how much I've fallen in love with a certain green-eyed blonde.'

Claire smiled when his lips found hers.

Epilogue

Two months later

The *Kimberley Adventurer* approached the mouth of the Norman River. Don stood behind Claire, his arms linked loosely in front of her. Sean had stayed on board when he'd left the boat in the marina at Darwin and flown to Sydney with Claire.

'Nervous?' Don's breath warmed her cheek as he lowered his head and brushed a kiss across her cheek.

'Very,' she said.

Don's chest vibrated against her back as he chuckled. 'This is from the woman who just took on the biggest television producer in the country, told him to get the media to back off, and informed him who'd set her up.'

'That was different. This is your *family*.'

If it wasn't for the nerves playing havoc with her, Claire would have been totally content. Thanks to a directive from the owner of the network, she was no longer in the sights of the media. Don had been with her every step of the way. They'd gone to Ben's house and Claire had fronted Giselle who'd moved in with Ben when Claire had left town.

Even though Giselle denied that jealousy had motivated her actions, she had admitted to setting Claire up. The network wasn't doing anything about it, because the ratings had gone thought the roof, and Giselle had kept her job.

The producer had begged Claire to sign another contract, but she'd looked at Don and smiled. 'Thanks for the offer, but no. I'm going back into law. I'm setting up my own business in the north.'

'You've already met half the family: Matt and Jenni. And Leni.' Don let go of her, and called to Sean, pointing to the wharf near the building that had McDOUGAL'S FISH CO-OP on the rusty roof. 'Over there, mate.'

'Yes, but when I met Matt and Jenni, I was just the new neighbour, only in the Bay for a few weeks.'

'And when you meet Mum and Rick, and Dane and Jake, you'll be the new lawyer in town.'

Claire was quiet as the boat approached the wharf where a group of people and a small girl waited.

'And the new daughter-in-law and sister-in-law.' Claire looked down at the new rings on her left hand, still unable to believe that she and Don had married in Sydney before they'd flown back to Darwin. They'd toured from Darwin to Broome in the *Adventurer* after they'd returned, and she'd had the best honeymoon anyone could wish for.

Who needed the south of France when you had Don McDougal for a husband?

Don took her shoulders and turned her around to face him. His blue eyes shone as he looked down at her. Claire's chest swelled with love for this man—her man—and all her nerves disappeared as he smiled at her.

'Stop worrying, sweetheart.' His words vibrated against her lips as he sealed his words with a gentle kiss. 'How could they not love you?'

THE END

If you enjoyed meeting the Douglas family, Her Outback Haven, Dane's story, is the third one in this series…

Dane McDougal has purchased land to build a luxury fishing lodge at a remote beachside location on the Gulf of Carpentaria. Reclusive potter and single mother, Nicole Curtis, has a three-year lease with the former owner. Dane was unaware that the house had a tenant, and he expects her to move out. Nicole digs her heels in, fearing for their lives if she and four-year-old Binnie have to move from this house in the wilderness.

Can Dane remain immune to the gentle charms of this woman and convince her to leave?

Have you read…

Come Back to Me

A beautifully written time travel love story. A romance that mixes the suspense and implications of time travel.

From award-winning author Annie Seaton, this romance over time will warm your heart.

Megan Miller has come to a crossroads in her career. Accusations of a breach of ethics in her university teaching have rocked her world. As she travels halfway across the world to the Glastonbury rock festival to research and complete her doctoral thesis, she hopes that the mess she leaves behind in Australia will be sorted while she is in England.

Davy Morgan, reclusive rock singer, tries to keep his music world and his private life separate; his very existence depends on it. But when the beautiful, fey woman turns up at the cottage next door, he must do all he can to keep his dark secret. Because everything is not as it seems in Davy's world.

When the truth comes out, can their love cross the decades, or will it be lost in time?

Also by Annie Seaton

Whitsunday Dawn
Undara
Osprey Reef
East of Alice (November 2022)

Porter Sisters Series
Kakadu Sunset
Daintree
Diamond Sky
Hidden Valley
Larapinta

Pentecost Island Series
Pippa
Eliza
Nell
Tamsin
Evie
Cherry
Odessa
Sienna
Tess

Also available in three boxed sets
Books 1-3
Books 4-6
Books 7-10

The Augathella Girls Series
Outback Roads
Outback Sky
Outback Escape
Outback Wind
Outback Dawn
Outback Moonlight
Outback Dust
Outback Hope

Sunshine Coast Series
Waiting for Ana
The Trouble with Jack
Healing His Heart
Sunshine Coast Boxed Set

The Richards Brothers Series
The Trouble with Paradise
Marry in Haste
Outback Sunrise
Richards Brothers Boxed Set

Bondi Beach Love Series
Beach House
Beach Music

ANNIE SEATON

Beach Walk
Beach Dreams
The House on the Hill

Second Chance Bay Series
Her Outback Playboy
Her Outback Protector
Her Outback Haven
Her Outback Paradise
The McDougalls of Second Chance Bay Boxed Set

Love Across Time Series
Come Back to Me
Follow Me
Finding Home
The Threads that Bind
Love Across Time 1-4 Boxed Set

Bindarra Creek
Worth the Wait
Full Circle
Secrets of River Cottage (Nov 22)

Four Seasons Short and Sweet
Ten Days in Paradise
Follow the Sun

Others
Deadly Secrets
Adventures in Time

HER OUTBACK PROTECTOR

Silver Valley Witch
The Emerald Necklace
Christmas with the Boss
An Aussie Christmas Duo (the two Christmas novellas)

www.ingramcontent.com/pod-product-compliance
Lightning Source LLC
Chambersburg PA
CBHW030640110726
47901CB00002B/511